Alma Fritchley was born in 1954 in a small market town in Nottinghamshire, and has lived in the Manchester area for the last twenty years. She is the author of the bestselling Letty Campbell series, which includes *Chicken Feed* (1998), *Chicken Out* (1999) and *Chicken Shack* (2000), all available from The Women's Press.

G000256122

Best

Alma Fritchley

Also by Alma Fritchley from The Women's Press:

Chicken Feed (1998)
Chicken Out (1999)
Chicken Shack (2000)

ALMA FRITCHLEY
chicken run

First published by The Women's Press Ltd, 1997
A member of the Namara Group
34 Great Sutton Street, London EC1V OLQ
www.the-womens-press.com

Reprinted 2000

British Library Cataloguing-in-Publication Data.
A catalogue record for this book is available from the British Library.

ISBN 0 7043 4691 5

Typeset in Plantin 11/12pt by Intype London, Ltd
Printed and bound in Great Britain by Cox & Wyman, Reading, Berkshire

This book is dedicated to Mum and Mariette

Acknowledgements

I'd like to thank my colleagues for their support and patience, especially Gail and Julie. Many thanks also to Michelle and Mick for their technical assistance. To Liz and Helen and the other members of The Junction Writers (and drinkers) Group, your encouragement was priceless. Thanks to everybody else – you know who you are.

But particular love and thanks to Eileen for keeping the faith.

Chapter 1

Erik's loud and horrible voice woke me, that and the sun burning into my eyeballs. My bed, that rock of ages, drew me insistently back into its welcoming depths. But Erik could not be denied.

Despite the sunshine, the floor in my lovely, sunny, south-facing pine bedroom was cold underfoot. Mind you, at six-thirty, even on a late summer's morning, what could I expect? The windswept moors of West Yorkshire were very different to the Manchester of my youth. It may have only been thirty miles to the south but in that small distance civilisation as I knew it had ceased to exist.

Erik screeched again, ending my reverie. I scuttled into the bathroom and prayed for hot water. Miraculously it was, hot that is. Sometimes it even failed to materialise at all. The pipes must have been installed at the turn of the century by a drunken Greek plumber. Not that I wish to slag off Greek plumbers, but after a visit to Lesbos a few years ago, the comparison seems to have stuck. Despite my moans I'm actually very fortunate, if a tad lonely (hence the complaining). This place hadn't cost me a penny. My old Aunt Cynthia left me the smallholding that has become my home.

At thirty I'd already given up any hope of becoming rich and famous beyond my own back yard. I still did the lottery of course, who doesn't, but out of the blue Old Cynthia had popped her clogs and left me her rambling house, a bit of land, and enough money to live comfortably, if carefully, for the rest of my life.

Assuming I didn't live until I was a hundred and twenty, of course.

Erik wasn't destined to live another five minutes.

I leaned out of the bathroom window and Erik, pausing in mid-croak, cast a beady eye in my direction. One avian foot paused in its descent. Erik, after Erik the Red because of his colouring and plumage, wasn't much in the brains department, but he knew when breakfast was due, and dinner, and tea. 'Shut up,' I hissed from my vantage point. He clucked in disgust in the time-honoured fashion of chickens. For he was indeed a chicken, a Rhode Island Red cockerel in fact, and his three preoccupations were feeding, fornicating (with several haughty chickens also left to me in Cynthia's will) and frightening the stray cat that sometimes made an appearance.

We regarded each other for a while and silently agreed to a ceasefire. He strolled off in search of Henrietta, a bandy-legged Pullet, his favourite chick of the moment, and I was left peacefully to my ablutions. Erik was lucky, I thought as I doused myself, for I had no chick of the moment with whom to occupy myself. I calculated the length of time it had been since I'd last got laid, never mind had a meaningful relationship. The chickens had more success than me. Not that I wasn't attractive, just isolated. And probably too damn choosy, I thought as I slipped on a pair of clean but time-worn jeans. Even out here I'd got wind of the latest lesbian chic fashions and the thought of chasing a lipstick lezzy

2

just didn't appeal. The thought of smelly chicken shit probably wouldn't appeal to them either. I giggled at the thought. The odd sound hung in the air, it needed an answering peal of laughter to make it sound right. God, I was getting morbid. Time for the radio and I tuned the battered Bush transistor to Radio 4. I was turning into my mother. Even worse, I was turning into Aunt Cynthia.

I was in time for the local weather report. 'The unusually dry spell will continue for the rest of the week and temperatures should reach a high of 20 Celsius, 70 degrees Fahrenheit' and on it went. I switched it off again before the national news could depress me. Droughts, wars and murders I could only stand once a week.

I finished dressing, I'd discarded my bra, the Queen probably wouldn't call today and my breasts could do with an airing. I galloped downstairs, breasts swinging happily in front of me, grabbed the chicken feed from behind the front door and proceeded to feed the brood. I was attacked from all sides. Erik and Henrietta led the pincer movement as I shook the dry, crumbly mixture into the metal troughs that passed as feeding bowls. The food was demolished in record time and my adopted family swanned off to contemplate another fun-packed day.

My own agenda was fairly empty. I had to clean the yard, of course, it was Wednesday (don't ask). Eggs would need collecting from the chicken run and I should have enough to warrant a trip to Calderton, the nearest village, and haggle for a price from Mrs Buckham, the old dear that ran the grocery shop.

As far as Mrs Buckham was concerned, Calderton was the centre of the universe and if only politicians would recognise this fact then the world would be a better place. It would certainly be a different place, that was for sure. If it was in the dust bowl of Kansas it wouldn't even graduate to 'hick town'. If I use the term 'red neck' to describe the inhabitants, you must realise I'm being generous. They'd been inbreeding since William the Conquerer was around.

I contemplated my neighbours as I swept and washed the yard. There had been much tut-tutting and twitching of nets when I'd first moved into the area a couple of years ago. I think Cynthia had left me the house and land out of malice. She had already let it slip that I was a dyke, in fact she'd embellished my life to such an extent I think they were expecting some kind of harem to arrive with me. Chance would be a fine thing. What they got was me, my girlfriend Julia (briefly), and my quirky and much-loved 2CV that didn't like hills, moors or rain. So soon there was just me. Julia, of sophisticated Italian descent, missed the city more than she missed me and the garaged remains of the car is now Erik's home and kingdom. It would be sad if I wasn't such a tough cookie. In ancient times I would have been named 'Letty the Stoic'. Nowadays just 'Letty the Olde Farte' would do.

I have a friend of sorts from the village, Miss Marple (no I couldn't believe her name either) and she runs the mobile library. We clocked each other the first time we met. Our common sexuality is never mentioned, of course, but I knew that she knew that I knew, if you follow. She's about ten years older than me but it might as well be fifty. My stereotyping was dashed though when I discovered she didn't live with another spinster lady. Instead she lives with her dead sister's daughter, AnnaMaria (all one word, rolls right off the tongue), a psychopathic sixteen-year-old that runs the librarian ragged. She's screwed more men than I've collected

4

eggs, and in two years that's a hell of a lot of eggs. Miss Marple can't keep up with her; it's not surprising she looks older than her years. I think she stuck with the librarian job as an escape from AnnaMaria, especially during the holidays. She's started college this year, and I bet Miss Marple's on her knees at this moment praying that it will calm her down, especially after AnnaMaria took the library van for a run. Ninety miles an hour down Death Gorge. How she didn't wipe out the whole of Calderton Village (it nestles at the bottom) escapes me. It's as well it ran out of petrol otherwise she'd be living in it in the South of France by now, probably selling library books on the side. It's a fascinating village isn't it? It's like *The Archers* on speed.

Miss Marple comes to visit me when her nerves are bad. I must be a calming influence. Still, after Anna-Maria a dog in the later stages of rabies would be calm by comparison. She brings me the latest lesbian thrillers, never says a word about them, just mutters that there are some new titles out she thinks I'll enjoy. She's right, lesbian PIs solving murder mysteries keeps at least one of my feet embedded firmly in reality. They also make me extremely randy. One sideways look and I'd be putty in some woman's hands.

My chores finally done, everything clean-washed, feather-free and eggs boxed, I pottered back into the kitchen to have a brew and, yes, you've guessed, an omelette, to keep mind and soul together. A couple of Henrietta's giant double yolkers quelled the screams from my stomach and I changed from my now filthy jeans into my favourite black 501s. Now I'm not a fashion victim by any stretch of the imagination, two years on a smallholding has made sure of that, but me and denim have a natural affinity and, optimist that I am, you never know who you're going to bump into, even in Calderton.

I'd flirted with the idea of seducing Miss Marple in one weak moment, but the mad niece had put me off. It would only have embarrassed the pair of us and for all I knew she was having a raving affair elsewhere.

I checked my appearance in the full-length pine mirror (Cynthia had a thing for blonde wood, the place was a conservationists' nightmare) and smiled at what I saw.

My hair is dark, very short with a spiky fringe. I'm a lesbian of the old school as you've probably gathered.

The local lads who help me clear my sizeable vegetable patch in summer always get a free hair cut with their pay packet. So I've made friends with the lads and an enemy of the hairdresser. I don't suppose you can win them all.

I tightened my belt a notch, I'd lost a few pounds recently, what with all the manual work I'd been doing (it still beats the mindless routine of insurance office work that I'd laughingly called a career).

The mirror told me what I already knew, I looked healthy, wealthy(ish) and desperate. No, too strong a term, eager was nearer. I put on my shades, imitation Ray Bans, but the locals would just think I'd got conjunctivitis. Briefly I debated going to Manchester, but the chickens would stop laying if their tea was more than ten minutes late and the effort of massaging their bruised egos was really too much. So I grabbed the keys to my Land Rover (a fairly new acquisition) balanced the trays of eggs in one hand and headed for the bright lights of Calderton Village.

Chapter 2

The phone greeted my return from my less than fruitful adventure. Mrs Buckham had shut up shop for the afternoon to visit her ageing and hypochondriac sister who lived nearby. I'd left the eggs in her backyard with a note attached suggesting an outrageous price that she could gossip about on her return. It was a game we played regularly, but I found that I quite missed the familiar routine of haggling over the price. What a very sad person I was getting to be.

I grabbed the plastic handset of the phone, Cynthia's concession to the modern world (she'd had it installed in 1974 and it was a vile two-tone brown affair) and yelled 'hello' into the mouthpiece. It was a little loud, I must admit, but it was the first time I'd properly exercised my tonsils all day. 'Shut up' and 'cluck, cluck' don't count. The phone hissed in protest, like stereo speakers too close together. This was followed by a thunderous silence. I tried again, this time my throaty hello sounded like Madame Chantreuse from the local knocking shop.

'May I speak to Letitia Campbell?' a snooty voice asked.

I was thrown for a second. No one called me by my

full name anymore, Cynthia had been the last to call me Letitia.

'Hang on, I'll see if she's in,' I squeaked, needing a moment to gather my thoughts. I cleared my throat and stamped up and down imitating footsteps and tried again in my more normal smokers' cough voice.

'Miss Campbell here,' I said. There, speaking could be effortless after all. 'How can I help you?' Underneath my countrified manner, an insurance clerk was trying to get out.

'Well, actually,' the snooty woman continued, 'it's how I can help you.'

'Look, I've got enough insurance to last me five life-times, thank you,' I said, mind still on the past. God, what a cheek, using hard sell on me! 'Or double glazing,' I added as an afterthought. The woman laughed mirthlessly, condescendingly, irritatingly. I was tempted to hang up but my voice cried out for more exercise.

'You misunderstand,' she said in a voice that would have put Einstein in his place. 'I'm not trying to sell anything.' Emphasis on the 'sell'.

'Well, what then?' I asked, down to earth, forthright manner back in its rightful place.

Unfazed by my words, she continued. 'I represent Steigel, Steigel and Blomquest.' She paused, expecting some sort of reaction from me, though I didn't know what. They sounded like the Swedish firm that had installed the three hundred acres of pine forest in old Aunt Cynthia's house.

'Of Manchester,' she added, as if I were dense and needed another hint.

'Is that Manchester, England?' I asked spitefully, and pointlessly. I heard her take a deep breath as if she were indeed dealing with an imbecile.

In those few seconds it took her to control her temper the names 'Steigel, Steigel and Blomquest' actually began to ring a bell.

I'd read something, or heard something about them recently, though I couldn't remember what. And then it hit me, though the knowledge was disappointingly banal. They were a group of auctioneers, a bit like Christies, but on a smaller and more regional scale. They specialised in cars, not just the older, rarer types, the Rolls-Royces and early marques of Jaguar and all the rest, but the modern, soon-to-be classic cars of the seventies and early eighties. I'd seen an article in *The Guardian* about the upsurge in interest. It had caught my eye because a 1966 Sunbeam Rapier, one of only seven or eight left in the country, had illustrated the article and my Dad had one like it before it was written off by some fool of a lorry driver. How Dad had walked away without a scratch was one of life's little miracles.

But then, what did they want with me?

Snooty drawers tried again. 'Well, Miss Campbell, we deal in . . .'

"Old cars,' I interrupted her, stealing her line and rattling her cage all at the same time. At that moment Erik the Red decided to leap on to the outside of the kitchen window and bellow loudly for his tea.

There was a sudden crash and an unladylike curse as the Receptionist from Hell dropped her phone in shock. I giggled and Erik squawked in reply. I opened the window with my one free hand and the fattest chicken in the North jumped clumsily into the sink, where he promptly drank noisily from my half-empty tea cup. At least it kept him quiet while Madam recovered her composure.

'Yes, old cars, classic cars,' she corrected herself. She

waited for me to get the point, when, quite frankly, there didn't seem to be one.

'I'm sorry,' I said forced to take the bait. 'I don't see what . . .'

It was her turn to interrupt. The whole conversation seemed to be made of half sentences, each of us clamouring to fill in the gaps. It was barmy and exhausting.

'Your name has been brought to our attention by a Miss Julia Rossi.' What has Julia been up to? I thought. We'd ended our relationship on friendly enough terms, though her job as an importer of foreign cars kept her busy. The connection struck me then. Honestly, the country life was making me a bit slow on the uptake.

'Oh yes,' I said, noncommittally.

'Well, unfortunately I can't really say too much on the phone, but I've taken the liberty of pencilling you in for an appointment with Steigel Senior. How does Friday at 3.30 sound?'

It sounded very peculiar actually, but curiosity overcame my dislike of the woman and I found myself agreeing. I clamped my hand over Erik's beak so I could catch the directions to their office. I even bade her a friendly farewell. I needn't have worried about the directions though, the office she mentioned was as familiar to me as the nose on my face. They'd taken over the lease on the property where my old insurance company used to be. I replaced the phone carefully and released Erik, who, outraged at my actions, shat in the sink and leapt, feathers aruffle, back into the yard.

Absently, I cleaned the sink and pondered the conversation. Julia's connection with Steigel etc. was clear cut, but the phone call had been anything but! I tried calling Julia's home but the breathy message on her answering machine suggested I call back later. Julia was hardly poor, but she had a curious reluctance to make BT any richer than they were already. Her work said she was out of the office until Friday, so the mystery would have to wait until then. The chickens wouldn't, so for the second time that day I endured their crowing to keep their tiny stomachs and tinier brains happy.

I pottered in the garden until the late summer's light started to fade, picked some tomatoes from the greenhouse to make something Italian for tea (Julia still had an effect) and retired to the homeliness and warmth of Cynthia's Scandinavian retreat.

Chapter 3

Thursday disappeared in a flurry of excitement and ruffled feathers. In a mad moment I decided to clean out Erik's throne, my rotting 2CV. It was parked at the back of the barn that also housed enough chicken feed to keep Bernard Matthew's lot happy. Cynthia, a war baby, had clung to the principles of hoarding, and her stores of dried and tinned food, jams and preserves, would see me through several nuclear holocausts.

I surveyed my car; it had seen much better days. I'd bought it in the seventies' quirky car boom when, at seventeen, I was the proud possessor of a full driving licence. I was also strictly vegan (run of the mill veggy now), a political lefty (still), and just discovering my lesbianism. And I'd got my insurance job. Life was amazing and I adored my car. It's just as well, because most of my wages were spent on keeping her going, especially towards the end of her days. I'd coaxed her into life every morning for almost fourteen years before West Yorkshire killed her off. Even then I couldn't bear to part with her, so as space wasn't a problem, she had been left to gather dust in a corner of my life. It's curious, but my Land Rover just doesn't evoke the same feelings as the 2CV and with this thought in mind and brush in hand, I surveyed 'Miranda's' remains.

Erik eyed me suspiciously as I edged my way past jars of peach jam and apple preserve. His head bobbed up and down watching my every move from the back seat of the car. The soft plastic top that was Miranda's roof, had, years before, decided to stick in the 'open' position and like it or not, in whatever weather, the car had become a permanent convertible.

Sunlight streaming through the barn's dusty windows glinted off Miranda's round headlamps. She'd been a classic car of sorts herself. Left-hand drive; the French number plate was still attached at the back, she was of the basic no frills design, built long before the Club version, with its pretence at sophistication, or the Dollys, with their happy two-tone colours, came along. She was grey, basic and old and I regretted my rash decision to confine her to the barn. With all the reminders of old cars, I was suddenly prompted into a nostalgia trip.

Erik proved to be a major obstacle and in the end I had to drag him off his nest by his scrawny neck and leathery legs. He batted me with his wings in protest but finally he stalked off complaining loudly to Henrietta whom he pecked for good measure. The end of a beautiful friendship, I suspected.

The state of the car defied description, but after the remains of Erik's dusty nest had been dumped on the compost heap, Miranda's true beauty began to emerge. She'd been sealed regularly when she'd been in running order so the rot, characteristic of 2CVs, hadn't set in, just a sad general air of decay.

In an inspired move during storage, I hadn't set the handbrake so, with a bit of effort she rolled easily through the back doors of the barn into the sunny yard beyond.

It's surprising what a good clean and polish will do. When I'd finished, a couple of hours later, there was the ghost of the car that had rolled off the production line in Paris in 1962. The soft top had defied my efforts at unravelling and instead had come apart in my hands. It would be easy enough to get a replacement I thought, fired with enthusiasm.

The engine, unfortunately, was beyond my expertise. Even after I'd charged up the battery, changed the plugs and points, she was still dead as a do-do. I spent twenty minutes yanking fruitlessly on the starter handle when a voice frightened the living daylights out of me.

I turned, clutching the starter handle (memories of living in inner city Manchester hadn't altogether left me) and I whirled on AnnaMaria, Miss Marple's gum-chewing niece.

'What?' I said still wielding the weapon.

'The car,' she repeated. 'What's up with it?'

Miss Marple came rushing round the corner of the barn at that point, pale faced and apologetic. 'I'm sorry, I had to bring her in the van with me today,' she began.

AnnaMaria was unfazed by her aunt's apologies for her and instead peered moodily into the car's engine.

'Won't it go?' she asked. I shook my head and, rather embarrassed, put the starter handle back into its rightful place.

'It's gorgeous,' she said, suddenly overawed by Miranda's gleaming bodywork. 'Do you mind if I have a go?'

Both Miss Marple and I nearly passed out at Anna-Maria's polite question. It was so unlike her.

'Help yourself,' I said and couldn't help but add, 'Don't break anything.'

14

She laughed and, rolling her shirt sleeves up, gently began to tinker with the car's innards. Miss Marple beckoned me away.

'Leave her to it,' she whispered as she led me sweatily away. 'It's her latest interest, keeps her out of mischief.'

We passed the library van parked at the side of the house as I took Miss Marple into the kitchen for a cup of tea. I kept an ear open for any sounds of AnnaMaria as I dumped tea bags into the pot and put the kettle on the hot ring of the Aga.

'Have you got some new books for me?' I asked, following the time-honoured game we played. She blushed, another ritual, and, to my surprise, shook her head.

'Well, no,' she stammered slightly. Her blush deepened and I turned to the sink and faffed about with sugar and milk to give her time to get to the point.

'It's about another matter.' I 'ohed' noncommittally. 'You see I've got this friend.' I dropped a spoon and held my breath.

'Oh, yes?' I said, still with my back to her.

'And I was wondering . . .'

The back door burst open and an oily AnnaMaria walked into the kitchen wiping her hands on a rag. God save me from sixteen-year-olds. 'Can I use the phone?' she asked. 'I want to ring Andy. I'm going to need his toolbox.'

'Help yourself,' I said and pointed to the phone. 'Who's Andy?' I mouthed to Miss Marple as Anna-Maria mumbled quietly down the phone.

'Current boyfriend,' she mouthed back, her colouring back to its normal state.

'He'll be up in a bit,' AnnaMaria cheerfully informed us as she disappeared into the yard.

'You were saying, Miss Marple?' I handed her a cup of tea.

'Please, call me Anne,' she said. At last, after two years.

I cleared my throat and took a seat opposite her. 'Anne,' I corrected and added, 'Letty.' We shook hands formally, as if we'd never met before and we laughed at the ludicrous situation. A whole iceberg crumbled at our feet. I waited for her to continue as she battled with embarrassment. 'Your friend?' I prompted.

'Yes, Caroline, she's my . . .' She fought for the right word, 'friend,' she finished lamely. And then suddenly it all came out in a rush. 'I know you've got connections in Manchester.'

Connections? It sounded like the Mob.

'And I've not been for years and Caroline's only young.'

Oh, yes?

'And she doesn't know Manchester very well, so we were wondering if, next time you go, of course, if we could possibly beg a lift off you. We'd pay for petrol, obviously.' She trailed off.

I was beginning to wonder why they didn't get the train like everybody else, when she added 'We thought we'd make a weekend of it, see the sights but we really don't know where to go.'

The 'really don't know where to go' spoke volumes.

'Right,' I said slowly, dragging the word out. It never failed to amaze me in this day and age, with the advent (and sudden demise) of Beth and her various lovers on *Brookside* and a variety of Lipstick Lezzies on *Eastenders*, that the gay message still didn't get across. We were thirty miles from one of the country's biggest gay communities but Anne Marple may as well have been living in Tibet.

16

'Can I use the loo?' she asked abruptly and she nipped upstairs as I shouted directions. AnnaMaria, oilier than ever, pottered back into the kitchen.

'It was my idea, you know?' she said airily.

'What?' I asked confused.

'To come and see you,' she said plonking herself at the table. 'Look, the whole world knows you're a dyke,' she said, Miss Sophisticate herself. 'And Auntie Anne's farted about for so long it was time she did something about it.'

I didn't comment, I doubt if I'd have got a word in edgeways anyway, AnnaMaria was on a roll. 'And then she met this Caroline on one of her library trips to Ribblethwaite. I caught them fumbling on the settee after I'd been to the pictures last Thursday. Auntie Anne nearly dropped cork legged and Caroline was no better. She's about twenty-five,' she added conspiratorially.

AnnaMaria obviously thought Caroline was ancient and Anne told me she was 'only young'. Odd isn't it?

'Anyway,' she continued, really into the story by now, 'I pretended I'd not seen them and I shoved Andy into the front room, but he's a bit gormless anyway and wouldn't have noticed. Gorgeous bod though.' She was thoughtful and I assumed she meant Andy and not her Auntie Anne. 'But the next morning I caught Anne crying in the sink so I gave her a real pep talk.'

I bet.

'I told her she couldn't hide her feelings forever and it was nothing to be ashamed of. It's all the rage in some parts, but she didn't believe that, she never watches telly you see. So I said she was to come and see you and get herself sorted out. There's loads of women out there. I mean Caroline's all right but she's a bit dim and auntie

17

could do a lot better for herself. So, what do you reckon?'

I reckoned that AnnaMaria would do well applying for a job as agony aunt in some provincial newspaper. The toilet flushed before I was forced to answer and AnnaMaria left the room with a satisfied smile. Anne was composed and looked ready to meet her maker when she reappeared.

'It's funny you should ask, about Manchester I mean,' I tried for reassurance. 'I'm off myself on Friday, I've got a meeting in town and I'll be spending the evening with my friend Julia, I think you met her once.'

I let that sink in before I went on. Anne's eyes brightened.

'I know a couple of bars that you'd perhaps enjoy. One is above a hotel, I'm going to stay there and I could book another room for you and your friend if you like. It's called Diva's,' I added.

She nodded eagerly. Actually the bar and hotel would probably be an ordeal by fire for Anne, if AnnaMaria's gossip had been true. Still it was the best place to stay and the bar was the busiest in town on a Friday. I didn't know what she'd make of the leather queens that frequented the male bar downstairs or the men in frocks that used the hotel rooms as walk-in wardrobes. I suddenly had a feeling she'd rather enjoy herself.

'That would be wonderful,' Anne said as a dozen expressions played across her face. A motorbike roared up at that moment and Andy with the gorgeous bod parked up outside my window. I'd not had so many visitors for ages. Talk about drought and flood.

He waved to Anne and nodded to me and lugged a giant tool box round to AnnaMaria who was immersed in the intricacies of French machinery.

'Look, I'm going to have to go,' Anne said. 'Caroline's waiting for me in Ribblethwaite, I've got some new titles for her.'

Preferential treatment, eh?

'Would it be all right to leave AnnaMaria and Andy here? They look happy enough at the moment.'

Indeed they did, AnnaMaria's dark locks and Andy's Bon Jovi mop were buried under the bonnet. I smiled, 'Yes, of course you can. I'll ring you later about Friday and confirm the booking, it shouldn't be a problem.'

Anne breathed a sigh of relief. 'Thanks ever so much,' she began, but I waved her thanks aside before she got embarrassed again. I watched her drive off and then set about making sandwiches for my hard-working mechanics.

By six o'clock I was knackered. Running about after the pair of them as well as all my other myriad jobs had worn me out.

I'd remembered to book the hotel rooms and I phoned Anne to give her the good news. She could hardly contain herself and I told her I would pick them both up outside the Post Office in Calderton at midday. That would give me plenty of time to get there, book in and get ready for my mysterious meeting.

AnnaMaria and Andy finished around seven and Andy mumbled about parts he'd need to finish the job. I was halfway impressed, I would be really impressed if Miranda ever ran again, and I slipped the pair of them twenty quid for their efforts. They asked if they could come back the following day for another go. I was too intrigued to say no. They also promised to feed the chickens too and I knew they would be safe in Anna-Maria's animal-loving hands. Despite previous experiences I was getting to like the young woman. It also saved me the job of persuading old George from the nearest farm to see to the hens.

I watched a few minutes of the ten o'clock news before my body craved sleep. Six-thirty would come around all too soon.

Chapter 4

I picked Caroline and Anne up as arranged at twelve. They had two suitcases each, perhaps they weren't planning on coming back. But I kept my thoughts to myself.

Caroline certainly wasn't the yokel I'd been expecting, just a normal young woman with fair hair wearing Levis and a white T-shirt. I eyed her leather jacket approvingly. Anne had the air of a woman who'd tried on fifty different outfits before, exasperated, she'd settled for smart blue slacks and a grey blouse. Her hair wasn't in its customary bun and instead lay in a loose ponytail down her back. She looked years younger, much nearer her actual age.

We chatted shyly for the first few miles. It wasn't easy to talk over the Land Rover's roaring diesel engine, but we managed. As I slipped into the fast lane of the M62 heading to town Caroline, who'd chosen to sit next to me, popped a tape into the fancy Blaupunkt stereo, the vehicle's only luxury, and Melissa Etheridge asked us if it was so hard to satisfy our senses. We were uncomfortably enthralled for the last ten miles of the journey.

The traffic in town was foul, as usual, and after parking the Land Rover in the municipal car park opposite, we dragged the luggage into the open doorway

21

of our hotel. A beefy weightlifter of a bouncer greeted us. Six feet four and sixteen stone, he looked like he could have eaten us for breakfast, luggage and all.

And then he opened his mouth.

'Are you the party from Yorkshire?' he squeaked, his voice somewhat at odds with his image. I nodded and he helped carry the bags to our rooms. Well actually, he carried them all, in one go. 'Anything you want, give us a scream,' he said. 'You can sign in when you come down,' he added. We must have looked trustworthy. Our rooms were next to each other and despite the sweaty leather queens milling about, you would have thought Anne was staying at the Ritz to hear her enthuse. My chintzy and pleasant room looked out onto the Chicken Take Away opposite. I felt a pang for Erik, though his body was safe in my hands. It wasn't the best view in the world but it wasn't the most expensive either. It suited me fine.

I changed from my faded jeans into the outfit I'd brought for the visit to Steigel, Steigel and Blomquest and went downstairs for a drink. I bypassed Anne and Caroline's room, the 'Do Not Disturb' sign was up already and envy touched me briefly. Still, you never know what a weekend would bring.

I bought a Budweiser and signed in and the receptionist/clerk/owner advised me to move my car to the tiny private car park at the back of the hotel. Finishing my drink first, I went and shifted the Land Rover, knowing I wouldn't need it again that day. Steigel's office, a smart address on Deansgate, wasn't far and I'd be able to window shop on the way. I left a short note for Anne and Caroline, should they emerge again that day and set off purposefully into town.

The rent boys and girls around the bus station barely gave me a second glance. For a Friday afternoon business was slack and I felt as safe as I did anywhere (except perhaps in Calderton) as I walked past the huddled groups.

Chinatown was busy, though, and my stomach did a grumble as I walked under the Arch and took in the sights and smells. Lunch could wait, it was almost three anyway and I wanted a quick look in Kendal's food hall. I was disappointed, hopes of the choice of food available were quickly dashed. Perhaps Lewis's would be a better bet later in the day.

Finally, I found myself outside my old insurance office. It had certainly been spruced up a bit since the Co-Op had shut up shop and amalgamated with Head Office on Miller Street. A brass plaque, newly polished and gleaming, proclaimed Steigel, Steigel and Blomquest's (of Leeds, Halifax and Manchester) existence. There was no clue on the door as to what they were about, though of course I was already privy to that information. I pushed open the solid door and took a deep breath before I entered the room marked 'Reception'.

Julia was happily ensconced on the receptionist's desk handing out a Gauloise when I appeared. Lounge Lizard sprang to mind. She hopped off the desk when she saw me. I'd not seen her for six months or more and somehow she looked – sleeker. She was always a cool dude, a classy woman who at thirty-eight looked classier still. Those smoky grey eyes had caused many an innocent to drop their drawers. Even old po-face behind the receptionist's desk looked shell-shocked. It never mattered to Julia if they were gay, straight or indifferent, if they were women, there was always a glimmer of hope.

I don't know how I ended up with her in the first

place, I thought as I took in Julia's devastatingly good looks. Her grey suit, all hand-made Italian silk by the look of it, fitted her like a second skin. Her black curly hair was swept into perfection behind the cute pierced ears. k. d. lang before she went femme. She'd always had money to burn, but now she looked as if she lit her fags with fivers.

'You came then?' she asked needlessly as she assessed me. Perhaps similar thoughts were running through her mind, though my dark green M and S pants and sharp white shirt didn't hold a candle to her outfit. I nodded and smiled and her arms were round me in a jiffy. She even smelt expensive as an overdose of Caroline Harrera's 'Harrera for Men' caught me unawares. The tanned skin of her neck was cool against my face.

A rattle of expensive electronic wizardry caused us to part and Jocelyn, as the receptionist name tag implied, tried to exert some control over the situation through the cloud of Gauloise smoke from her cigarette. 'If you'll just take a seat,' she demanded, 'I'll notify Steigel Senior that you've arrived.'

I half expected the wallpaper to cascade off the walls as her paint stripper voice loudly filled the room.

However, she did no such thing. I was ten minutes early and it was quite clear that I would have to wait for my allotted appointment. Julia grabbed my hand and I could feel the pressure of gold against my fingers as she led me to a leather sofa as far away from Jocelyn as she could get.

She fluffed up a cushion for me before I could stop her, Casanova could have taken lessons. 'Cut the crap, Julia,' I muttered as I gave myself up to the comforts of Olde Worlde England.

She sat sideways on, her back to the chain-smoking receptionist and facing the carved oak door from which

Steigel Senior would make an entrance. Julia's eyes were burning with some knowledge that I had no party to, she was fidgeting and strangely silent, which wasn't like her. I wondered momentarily what she was on, but just as quickly dismissed the thought. She was a lover of mellow Scottish malt and the occasional smelly French cigarette. She was as far removed from drugs as Mother Theresa. Now I know Julia sounds an unlikely candidate for *Farmer's Weekly* and I nearly had a seizure when she said she'd come with me to the country, but she'd tried wellies on for size for six months, though the reality hadn't fitted her ideal. Classic Cars had welcomed her back with open arms, she was the best salesperson they'd ever had, and I'm sure she'd dined out on *Country Life* stories for months. I missed her for a while but it was never really meant to be, and Erik had hated her. Secretly, I think when he and Henrietta had adopted her open-topped Mercedes coupé as a love nest, it had been the final straw.

Julia was no ordinary, wealthy dyke-about-town. From monied parents and private education to a position she had real talent for, it was obvious she was never going to be a chicken lover. And where did I fit into this fast lane? She'd liked my humour and fancied my mother to whom she'd sold one of the last Beetles to be imported from Belgium, but had settled for mum's look-a-like, me.

The Volkswagen had been a bargain and had been bought with the insurance money from Dad's death. Mum still drives it and chugs over to see me occasionally from her adopted Macclesfield.

Anyway, that's how we met, how it progressed and how it ended. Our relationship condensed into a couple of paragraphs. The telling was as exhausting as the loving.

25

Julia was watching me carefully. 'Well?' I said. 'What gives?'

She grinned, her eyes, the edge of nervousness gone, were mischievous and dimples appeared on both cheeks. Was there any wonder I'd fallen for her? Me and a thousand others.

Before she could answer, the inner sanctum of Steigel Senior's office was revealed and Steigel Senior herself appeared in the doorway. Julia leapt to her feet and in that sudden movement all was revealed. Julia leapt to her feet and in that sudden movement all was revealed. Julia was wonderfully, newly, ecstatically in love, probably truly for the first time in her life, and who could blame her?

Steigel Senior was a cool-eyed, blonde-haired Lauren Bacall, complete with Dietrich's mystery and Garbo's gorgeous accent. If I'd been a politico and not a film buff, she'd have had Hilary Clinton's looks and Barbara Castle's charm. But I knew in an instant that Julia's feelings were not reciprocated.

Steigel beckoned us into her sumptuous office. 'Jocelyn,' she commanded, 'no interruptions, please. You'll have to excuse her I'm afraid,' Steigel Senior said as she closed the door, 'she's rather new to the firm.'

Her accent was clipped, Scandinavian perhaps, and her voice mellow. I could almost hear her whispering sweet nothings. She smiled and gave us her full attention; the face that launched a thousand ships. Her hair was expensively streaked and in a style so modern, nobody had thought of it yet. Ms Steigel was gracefully tall, aged anywhere between thirty-five and forty-five, with a lived-in elegance she'd been born into rather than acquired. Julia looked on adoringly and Steigel blessed her with a warm and knowing smile. She

26

reached out, took my hand and squeezed it gently. I felt more expensive gold against my skin.

'Ms Campbell,' she said, and added without a trace of insincerity, 'I'm so glad you could come. Please take a seat.'

I edged into a delicate Queen Anne chair and resisted the impulse to check for its authenticity. I had a feeling it wasn't a copy. Julia sat to one side on its twin and Ms Steigel took her regal place behind the obligatory oak desk left over from a long ago age of prosperity.

Unsurprisingly, though jarringly at odds with the decor, framed prints of cars from past eras adorned the walls. I recognised the boxy shape of a Model-T Ford, the elegant ostentatiousness of a 60s' Thunderbird convertible, all bright red and chrome. There were Silver Ghosts of days gone by and, to my surprise, a replica of my own Miranda.

My attention was drawn back to Ms Steigel who was waiting patiently for me to finish my perusal.

'Sorry,' I said.

She smiled. 'They're beautiful, aren't they? Julia told me you had some interest in the classics.' I was surprised at her comment. My interest after all was fairly minimal. I didn't know that much about them and anybody, surely, would love the models that graced her walls. I said as much to her.

'You'd be surprised, Ms Campbell, how many people are happy to drive around in today's expensive tin cans and not have the imagination to make a sound investment for the future.'

Bloody hell, I'd pressed the wrong button.

She laughed, a warm full sound, as though surprised at her own reaction. 'I'm sorry,' she said, blue eyes fired with enthusiasm. 'It's my hobby as well as my job.' She

27

paused. 'Can I offer you a drink? I believe you've had a fair drive down.'

Odd that she knew I'd driven, but I suppose in her line of business she assumes that everyone over the age of twelve drives everywhere.

'Yes, please,' I said. 'A coffee will be fine.'

'Your usual, Julia?' she asked, and Julia nodded gormlessly.

Ms Steigel left the room, presumably to put some life into Jocelyn. 'How long has this been going on?' I hissed at Julia as soon as Ms Steigel was out the door.

'About six months,' she hissed back. 'Isn't she drop-dead gorgeous?'

Ms Steigel came back into the room before I could reply and I could hear Jocelyn rattling about in the background. She handed a tumbler of whisky to Julia as she returned to her seat. Ice clinked against the Waterford crystal. The scenario was getting better and better, I was far too fascinated to feel nervous.

'You're probably wondering why I wanted to see you?'

What an opening line, I thought, as Jocelyn sneaked up behind me and banged my coffee down on the desk. Her accompanying smile would have frightened Attila the Hun. She obviously hadn't forgiven me for our telephone conversation earlier in the week. I thanked her sweetly and gazed back at the enchanting features of Ms Steigel.

'Well, I'm curious,' I admitted. She reached into a drawer and placed an A4 folder on her spotless and uncluttered desk.

'I've a proposal to make, Ms Campbell, that I think you may find appealing.' She paused for effect. I wanted to grab her and shake it out of her but I took a gulp of my coffee instead. It was disgusting, but I could hardly spit it back into the cup. I swallowed with some effort. Jocelyn, I'll get you for that one day.

I looked across at Julia. Her composure had quite escaped her and a flush had darkened her already dark skin. She had one thing on her mind and it wasn't Ms Steigel's proposals, not this one anyway.

I nodded for the executive to continue. 'I understand you own a smallholding in the West Riding, a piece of land left to you by your, er . . .' she consulted her folder, 'aunt on your mother's side.'

It wasn't so surprising that Steigel had access to this information. Julia had never been famous for keeping her lip zipped.

'I don't know whether you know, but this particular piece of land has potential rather greater than the chicken farm you run at present.'

Light dawned. 'Ms Steigel,' I said frostily, 'before you go on, my land is not, and will never be for sale. My aunt farmed there for longer than I care to remember.'

My back was up, she was messing with the wrong woman. I glared at Julia, who was staring nonchalantly at the traffic beyond the window.

'You misunderstand,' Steigel said hurriedly. 'I'm not proposing to buy it, although I would be prepared to offer a six-figure sum, should you ever change your mind.' She paused and waited for a response, she got one from Julia who looked around in surprise.

'No, for the moment I'm offering you a chance to lease part of your land on a short-term basis.'

I opened my mouth to protest, I didn't like being bullied and Julia's girlfriend was getting dangerously close. She held up her hand to silence me, accompanying the gesture with a disarming smile. 'I believe you have two acres lying fallow at the moment and to be honest they would be ideal for our purposes.

29

I'm sorry if I've given you the wrong impression. A short-term lease of say, two months, would be sufficient. The rewards could be quite substantial,' she added.

'What exactly are your requirements?' I asked; after all there was no harm in asking. She leaned back in her leather chair.

'We intend to set up the North's largest open-air classic car auction. Should the proposal be acceptable, Julia has agreed to set up the deal, with backing from her own firm Classic Cars PLC and financed initially by this office. Now, you may wonder why I have your piece of land in mind. Geographically it is ideally suited, your land is sound, with good drainage and it's unused at the moment. We can guarantee it would be returned to you undamaged.'

My mind spun in an effort to keep up. True, my home was fairly central to visitors from Leeds and Manchester, and all the big northern cities had good motorway access. But so did a lot of other places; there was no shortage of farmland.

I pointed out this fact, I'm not stupid.

'The thing is,' Julia piped up for the first time, 'it would be a favour to me.'

'Oh, why?' I asked and, turning to Julia, was surprised by her look of pleading. Her hands shook and she put down her glass of whisky.

'Well, to be honest,' she said clearing her throat, 'I'm in a bit of a quandary with work at the moment. I've made a few, erm, errors of judgement lately and I need the deal to get me back on track.'

'Pretty vague, Julia, get to the point.'

'The truth is,' she began, though I was beginning to suspect that I wouldn't hear the truth at all, 'we've been lumbered, well, I've been lumbered with cars that I can't shift. I've been caught with my pants down and I need a blockbuster of a sale, the biggest, the one that will draw people from London, the States, Japan, people who have the money to get the firm moving again. This firm can produce a couple of headturners that should get buyers here in the first place and with the cars I've got in stock we should make a turnover of . . .'

'Hang on, Julia,' I said. 'Don't get too technical, life is short enough as it is, but what I can't understand is why you are taking all this on your own shoulders. No disrespect, but you're just a saleswoman, the buck doesn't stop with you, that's why you've got management for God's sake.'

'That's the point, you see,' she said. 'I am management now. I'm principal director of Classic Cars. The firm was shaky over last winter and I bought them out. It took every penny I had, even a loan from Dad. Everything I've got is invested in it. And then Simone here,' she indicated Steigel Senior, 'came up with this idea. It could really work well. You've got the land, I've got the cars and Simone's got the money.' The excitement was back in her eyes, accompanied by an odd air of desperation.

'What's the catch?' I asked. I'd seen too many films not to know there had to be one somewhere.

'The catch, Ms Campbell,' Simone Steigel came back into the conversation, 'is that there would be no money up front. The deal is that money to pay for leasing your land would come after the sale had been set up and executed.'

She leaned over the desk and pushed the folder toward me. 'Our proposals are in here. Obviously I don't expect an immediate answer. I'm sure you have many questions for Julia. Please, I'd like you just to

31

think about it for now. Ideally I'd like to be in a position to advertise while we have weather on our side. That gives us, you, just a couple of weeks before we have to consider an alternative and two months before Julia has to face possible closure and all that that can entail,' she said obscurely. 'I know it's not much time and I hate to pressure you but that's how things stand at present.'

I took the folder from the polished desk. I had no idea Julia was in such dire straits. Her family would have a fit if she ended up in a debtor's court. The folder contained a fairly straightforward contract, one which could easily be checked by my mother. She's worked for a solicitor's for years. The drawings and graphs, estimated figures and overheads also contained in the folder were too technical to take in at a glance.

Simone came round the desk and sat on its edge. She held Julia's hand, the first signs of affection I'd seen and she smiled warmly into her eyes. Julia looked as though she would burst into tears and I found myself reaching for her other hand. I couldn't help it, I'm such a soft git.

'Look, Julia, I'll study your folder and have a word with Mum. I can only promise to think about it. I wish you'd told me what had happened, you're too damned proud for your own good.'

Julia shrugged and a tear tumbled down her cheek. She brushed it away angrily. I got up to leave and slipped the folder into my bag.

'I'll see you out,' Julia said.

I shook hands with Simone. I really didn't know what to make of her. She seemed genuinely fond of, if not desperately in love with, Julia, and the firm seemed to be on the level, judging by their premises and from what I could remember of the newspaper article.

Promising a drink later at the bar, Julia firmly in

butch role opened the door for me, just in time to catch old Jocelyn scurrying back to her desk. Caught in the act of nosiness she blushed and pretended to sort papers.

'Thanks for the coffee, dear,' I simpered as I went past. Julia, so in love, missed the encounter and imagined I was being particularly pleasant. But Jocelyn's card was marked. It took me a few minutes to get over the encounter, come to terms with all the twists and turns in my life, but I couldn't help feeling a modicum of excitement at these latest events. After all, I'd been missing a few thrills lately. I giggled to myself. From chicken farmer to wheeler dealer in the space of two days.

I couldn't wait to tell Anne.

Chapter 5

After the meeting I dallied a while in King Street, the poshest end, and sated my appetite with a cheese filled croissant from the French sandwich shop.

I'd had a bash at Steigel's proposals sat propped between a leathery bag lady and a pale, stressed City man who was mumbling nervously into a mobile phone. If I'd been asked to choose to live as either one, I'd have been hard pressed to make a decision.

The legal speak of Simone's proposals had left me brain dead and no wiser. I was a chicken farmer, not an articled clerk, so, exasperated, I shoved the folder back into my rucksack. She'd said I had to make a decision fairly quickly so I might as well make the most of the time I'd got. I'd also do well to take advantage of my weekend in Manchester. With that thought I left the city-centre bench to the bag lady and the sweating gent and headed back to the hotel.

Anne and Caroline had emerged from their siesta when I got back about four. The city, and in particular the Gay Village, was already teeming with life. Surprising how a spot of sunshine will empty the closets. My newfound friends were deep in conversation at the bar and I ordered myself another Bud and dry white wine for them. I grimaced as I thought what state their stomachs would be in come morning, but as I placed their drinks in front of them realised they wouldn't have noticed if they were drinking drain cleaner.

'Was your meeting all right?' Anne asked politely, reluctant to gaze at anything but Caroline. I gave them a shortened version of events to date. Caroline was fascinated and encouraged me to 'go for it' more than once. Her enthusiasm was very encouraging. Anne was rather more cautious. Perhaps years spent as a librarian had dulled her sense of excitement.

Caroline offered to look at the deal, she'd got a first in one of the sciences and some business qualification at pre-University Huddersfield Poly; not quite as dim as AnnaMaria would have me believe. I shrugged and handed the folder over and she pored knowledgeably over the draft of the contract and all the squiggly mathematical jargon the folder contained. Defeated, Anne turned to me for conversation.

'And how do you like it so far?' I asked her with a smile.

She laughed, gone was Miss Marple, Librarian, replaced by Anne, lover of women with worlds to conquer. I was beginning to suspect that her sense of excitement wasn't quite so dulled after all. Her severity had been softened, either by Caroline's ministrations and laying on of hands or the wicked wine she'd been putting away.

'I can't wait for tonight,' she said, eyes lighting up at the thought.

'Oh, yes?' I said quietly, loading the question. She slapped my arm playfully and blushed. Caroline was blissfully unaware of the wordplay. We decided to eat at a nearby Italian restaurant. Caroline wasn't consulted.

'She'll eat anything,' Anne assured me. 'But I really wanted to do a bit of shopping before then, do you think we've got time?'

I checked my watch, 4.30. 'Depends what you're after,' I said.

'Well, a pair of jeans really,' she said shyly. 'For tonight.'

I could sympathise with that.

'And I wanted my hair cut.'

I looked at her long thick locks in surprise.

'It's been down my back for so long,' she said hurriedly, 'I thought it was time for a change. Can you recommend anyone?'

Well, I usually recommended myself but thought she probably wouldn't appreciate being scalped. 'The nearest and cheapest hereabouts is the Village Hair shop, look, you can see it from here.' I pointed through the open door. 'They're pretty quick, too, if they're not busy, gives you time to get some jeans. Is Caroline going with you?' Caroline looked up at the mention of her name. I explained about the shopping expedition.

'Would you really mind if I didn't go?' she asked Anne. 'This is really fascinating,' she said, waving the folder.

'No, that's fine,' Anne replied and turned hopefully to me.

'Do you want me along?' I asked.

'Please, if it's no trouble.'

It was okay by me, I didn't need much of an excuse to buy a pair of jeans. And maybe a new T-shirt to go with it.

We left Caroline, who'd gone in search of a phone, to it, and headed for the Village Hair shop. Mercifully it was empty when we arrived and though Anne suddenly got cold feet, she went anyway, to have her dark tresses clipped.

I buried my head in the gay paper *The Triangle*, thoughtfully left out for such occasions, and by the time I'd got to the Personals: 'Leather Dyke into whips seeks TLC and cuddles from similar(!)', Anne had been transformed. I barely recognised her. Her ears were showing, probably for the first time in thirty years and the soft crop, heavier on top, short at the back and sides, suited her features. She smiled, obviously thrilled by the change, and paid for the cut, tipping so heavily I thought the hairdresser would faint from shock.

We left the shop, Anne clutching a bag containing her hair. 'I saved it for Mum,' she confided. 'She swore she'd disown me if I ever had it cut. Let's see if she keeps her word.' She giggled ferociously.

I had no idea they were on such lousy terms but I kept my counsel; it was none of my business. Anne grinned all the way to the Arndale shopping centre and sneaked a look at herself in every shop window that we passed. I took her to 'World of Denim' and breathed deeply of the lovely, unmistakable smell. Anne looked bewildered, she didn't have a clue where to start. We politely waved away the assistant and Anne bravely put herself in my capable hands. She was taken by the stone-washed blues of the various American jeans (most of them made in Taiwan, but what the hell). Anne confessed she thought the button flies were daring and sexy, not a word she was used to using I thought. She was a size sixteen, easy enough to cater for, and in the end she couldn't decide which of three pairs she liked best. A pair of Lees, 501s and Pepes lay at her feet. She looked at me in consternation over the fake Western swing doors that swerved as entrance to the changing rooms.

37

'What do you think?' she asked me for the umpteenth time.

'You look great in them all,' I assured her, which she did, years were dropping off her by the second.

'That's it then,' she mumbled and disappeared from sight to re-emerge seconds later, wearing the Pepes. 'I'll have them all.'

She was likely to be bankrupt at this rate. She bought a leather belt at the counter and grabbed a packet of three black T-shirts for good measure.

We treated ourselves to a coffee in a tacky café nearby. Thrilled by our purchasers (I'd plumped for Levis), we discussed them and much else over our drinks.

The conversation took a serious turn.

'Letty,' Anne began, 'I really don't know how to thank you.' I opened my mouth to protest but her look stopped me. 'I mean it. I didn't realise how much your friendship could mean. We've known each other, what? Two years?'

I nodded.

'And yet in these few days, hours really, I feel as if I'm really getting to know you.' It was my turn to blush. I'd not had a conversation like this for a long, long, time.

'I don't think I could have continued my relationship with Caroline without your support. And AnnaMaria's too of course,' she added with a smile.

'Yes, she told me what happened.' I wanted to encourage her.

'I was mortified when she walked in on the two of us. It's all so new to me, though I'm not quite as ignorant as AnnaMaria seems to think.' She paused to gather her thoughts.

I was silent, her coming-out story was in the offing and I wanted to listen to what she had to say, to get a sense of her life and feelings. She was a truly genuine and warm woman. One that Caroline, or whoever she ended up with, would be lucky to have.

'I mentioned my mother earlier,' she said. 'And she really is as foul as I intimated. My father died when I was a child.'

I knew that much from conversations with Mrs Buckham from the grocer's.

'And Mum, who had always ruled the roost anyway, decided I would be the one to get the brunt of her bitterness. I looked altogether too much like Dad for her, and she was reminded of him everyday. As you can imagine, it was difficult for me.' She paused again and took a drink of the strong coffee. 'It took me years before I could leave home and then only to the next street. I'd still be living with Mum now if Diane, that's my sister, hadn't been killed in a car crash, and I offered to take on AnnaMaria. I'm not quite sure whether I've made a pig's ear of that or not,' she smiled. 'But at least she's loved and she can always come to me with her problems.'

'I think probably AnnaMaria's just a bit wild. I know I was at her age,' I added, remembering my own wilfulness. 'And she's certainly not daft by any means.'

Anne sat back in her chair and flicked at her hair. She looked surprised when it wasn't there to flick. She tentatively touched her scalp.

'You'll get used to it,' I advised. 'How did you meet Caroline then?' I asked, eager to know more.

'In Ribblethwaite,' Anne leaned forward once more. 'She got on the van, I park it behind the old bus station.' I wasn't sure what significance that had, but she went on, 'I can still remember what books she picked up. I was fascinated by her, even then. She had Forsyth's *Business Management Skills*, the latest Barbara Cartland

39

for her mum; some book on old cars. I noticed that because it's not been taken out for ages, and she was the second person to pick it up in a fortnight. And what really caught my eye was *Rubyfruit Jungle*, the first lesbian book I ever read.'

'It was mine too!' I chortled. 'I remember getting in a tiz when they had sex in the playpark.'

Anne giggled, 'Yes, so did I!'

'And then what?'

'Well,' she said taken by the telling. 'I felt ever so brave. I just asked her nonchalantly, like you do, the following week when she brought it back, if she'd enjoyed it. She said she had of course. I'd have gone right off her if she hadn't. So I suggested a few other titles she might enjoy. She'd already read a lot of them apparently. Nowadays I suppose three years at Poly opens your eyes a bit, but there were one or two she didn't know. I couldn't believe she hadn't read *The Well of Loneliness*. Still, it is a bit morbid. I'm glad I didn't discover that first, I'd have probably thrown myself in the canal.'

My laughter turned a few heads in the café and the proprietor scowled at me. She was obviously unused to mirth.

Anne leaned forward, she may have been rocketing out of the closet, but there were still a few pitfalls.

'So, anyway I offered to drop off any new titles that came along. She works in Halifax, you know, in a drugs company, so I'm not in Ribblethwaite when she gets home from work. Though to be honest I'd have gladly changed my routine to fit her in.'

'God!' I said. 'Can you imagine? The ladies of Calderton and Ribblethwaite would have been less shocked if the Pope had ruled that Mary wasn't a virgin.'

More cups rattled as we fell about at the joke. I wiped my eyes. I love making people laugh.

'Best of all,' Anne said recovering, 'she invited me for tea. We fell into bed after a good curry and a bottle of Mrs Buckham's home-made wine.' She paused. 'And I've never been as happy in my life.'

I reached for her hand, fuck the proprietor.

'It shows,' I said and gave her fingers a squeeze. Anne sighed and for a second she left her hand in mine.

'Shall we go?' she asked abruptly. 'I think they're ready to close and I'm dying to see what Caroline thinks of my hair.'

'She'll love it,' I assured her.

We collected our bags and, like a couple of old friends, chatted happily through the streets and headed towards the hotel.

Caroline thought her hair was fantastic.

Chapter 6

Simone's proposals had been pushed under my door when I got back. Caroline had thoughtfully tacked a note to it.

'Looks like a winner to me' she'd written.

> I understand your land is freehold so, if you can bear to lose it for a couple of months and take a risk, your one per cent cut should keep you in holidays for a couple of years. Nothing definite of course, it *is* a risk. But what isn't?
>   See you in the restaurant next door at seven.
>   Caroline.

Short, sweet and very encouraging I thought as I slipped into my sexy new jeans. A white T-shirt topped them off. Some woman's going to be lucky tonight I promised my reflection in the bathroom mirror. Think positive, my mother used to say. And then I remembered. Damn, she's off on holiday tomorrow, I'd have to find another legal eagle for the car thing. I pushed it to the back of my mind; I had better things to do at the moment. My stomach grumbled in anticipation.

First things first, food.

The restaurant was fairly new and already busy when the three of us arrived. Anne looked stunning in her new clothes, though her fancy sandals clashed a bit with her outfit. Perhaps I could gently point her in the direction of a decent shoe shop the following day. Or Caroline could anyway, she seemed very much at home with lezzy fashions. She still wore her leather jacket and jeans but her long-sleeved, off-the-shoulder T-shirt was a very sexy touch. Her shoulder-length, fair hair was on more than nodding acquaintance with dreadlocks; matted, Mum would have called it; modern, Anne would say. Too much like hard work for me.

Over dinner, vegetable lasagna for me, carbonara for the two of them, Caroline chatted unselfconsciously about her job at the drugs company; she was vague about what she actually did, though I got the impression it wasn't a particularly lowly position; and about life in general and her and Anne in particular. Every so often they'd link hands and it was really rather lovely to see, though envy was still perched on my shoulder. I took solace in food and demolished my pasta and two rounds of garlic bread. My chances of finding a woman tonight were diminishing by the minute. Still, my chance of food was a dead cert, the possibility of sex, knowing the cut and thrust of Diva's clientele, was slim at best.

We washed the meal down with a rough Italian red, not my usual tipple but I wanted to be sociable. Caroline mentioned the car deal over our third glass as the waiter cleared away the remains of our meal.

'It looks all right to me,' she said, swirling the liquid in her glass, 'but I wouldn't blame you if you got a second opinion.'

'I was going to get Mum to mull it over for me, but she's gone to the States for six weeks, so she'll miss the whole shenanigans. She works for Mee's, a solicitor's in Macclesfield, you know,' I explained.

'Actually I could offer you some help there,' Caroline shifted in her seat. 'My company works closely with a law firm in Halifax. We need them to help us get new products off the ground and legally we're required to meet certain legislation. It's all a bit complicated, not really my field. But anyway I could have a word, if you like. See what they think. It won't cost you anything, I can ask a friend from the department.'

I shrugged and said, 'Okay, if it's no trouble.' It may have been me, but somehow she looked relieved. I dismissed the thought and we turned instead to the evening ahead.

'I'm surprised you don't know Manchester, Caroline,' I said.

'Oh, I used to years ago.'

'It can't have been that many,' I said laughing. 'You're only, what, twenty-five?'

'Ah, yes,' she said with a smile. 'But I came out when I was sixteen.'

Anne nearly fell off her seat. 'Really?' she exclaimed. 'I had no idea.'

'You've got a lot to learn about me,' Caroline said, tapping the side of her nose.

'So you knew Manchester, what? Nine, ten years ago? What was it like then?' Anne asked. Caroline took a moment to think about it.

'Political,' she decided. 'And only a small scene then. I got bored with it. I'm not political, all those right-on feminist separatists got on my tits. Leeds had a good social life then, it still has and it's much more my style.'

I resisted an impulse to tell her that without 'right-on feminist separatists' we wouldn't have gained the small gains we have, but I didn't want to sound like an old fart, and so instead commented, a tad hastily, 'You'd like it now, then. Manchester, a hedonist's dream.' Suddenly the whole dynamic of the evening shifted a gear.

She regarded me carefully and I couldn't read her eyes at all. I changed tack, I didn't want a verbal sparring match at this stage and Anne looked uncomfortable. I didn't really know her views yet, either, but suspected they'd lean more towards my own.

'Have you thought about moving here?' I asked.

Caroline cleared her throat and drank her wine thoughtfully. 'No, I don't want to commute for hours every day. And I'd be too far away from Anne,' she added, squeezing her hand again.

We were careful not to mention politics again. It's always a minefield and I couldn't really be arsed. Apart from that she was doing me a favour and I wasn't prepared to cut my nose off to spite my face. Instead we talked music for a while and our tastes were similar enough to have a fair old discussion. Nina Simone was a good starting point and for someone who wasn't 'political' Caroline knew the woman's music back to front. She even had an album I didn't, which I would have thought would have been impossible considering the size of my record collection, and she promised to tape it for me.

We left the restaurant at ten, a time when I knew Diva's would be starting to fill. I got the same nervous stomach I always got when I was visiting a dykes' hang-out that I hadn't been to for a while. Though I'd had enough wine to run the gauntlet when all eyes turned to the door as someone new came in.

The place hadn't changed much, though of course it looked smaller than I remembered. By some miracle we managed to get a table a step ahead of a group of 'Femme to Femme' lookalikes.

Anne's eyes were on stalks, I felt positively jaded by comparison and Caroline was as cool as you like. There were no familiar faces. Somehow I always think I'm going to know everybody; it's funny how fast things can change and in two years the lesbian scene had changed beyond recognition.

Mercifully, Julia was five minutes behind us and of course she was a stranger to no one, eliciting admiring glances from the groups of women dotted about. She looked as delectable as she had done earlier in the day, though her clothes were a little more casual; expensively tasteful. Her slacks and shirt, muted colours of autumn, were from Gap, maybe French Connection, and she exuded her customary assurance.

She spotted me and came over immediately, dispensing 'hellos' on the way. She kissed me on the mouth. 'Mmm, garlic,' she said, lover of the stuff herself. She greeted Anne warmly, whom she knew slightly from her months spent living with me in the country, and shook hands rather formally with Caroline. Anne was pleased to see her, if a little bowled over by her charm, but Caroline was suddenly rather subdued. Julia seemed to have stolen her thunder somewhat, though I doubt that had been her intention.

To alleviate the odd tension that followed Julia's arrival, I dragged her to the bar and left the two women to get on with their 'love thang'.

'Behave yourself,' I muttered to Julia as we edged to the bar.

'What?' she said innocently, as she took a place by my side.

'You know what,' I said crossly. She looked blank. 'Those two,' I said indicating our table. 'It's new to

46

them, well Anne anyway. Don't be such an old smoothie.'

Julia laughed. 'She's nice, I like her. I know Caroline from somewhere too, though I can't place her. Anyway, what's with you and this mothering instinct?'

'I'll explain another time. Are you driving?'

'Nope, Simone's picking me up later. Said she'd call in if she had time.'

'It's serious then?' I asked as I waited to be served.

'Dunno, well yes, it is for me. I can't speak for Simone though, she's such a dark horse.'

I ordered a Bud, two glasses of wine and a Jameson's for Julia.

'Wait here,' I ordered. 'I want to hear it all.' I scuttled back to the two women who were already engrossed in each other and left the wine and them, to it. Julia was flirting with the bar staff when I returned, she couldn't seem to help herself no matter how much she professed to be in love. I dug her in the ribs to get her attention. It transpired, as we dawdled over our drinks, that Julia had met Simone the previous summer when she was on the verge of taking over Classic Cars. A fairly new firm, Steigel, Steigel and Blomquest had emerged on to the automobile scene in a blaze of publicity, in car circles at any rate. With money from rich pickings abroad they'd slipped neatly into a gap in the market brought about by new money moving into the North. These southern Tories had wanted fancy cars to go with their 'picturesque and rural' status symbol homes.

Julia had no qualms about taking their money and with her selling skills and Steigel's ability to import the right sort of cars at a good price they'd set up a lucrative partnership together. For a while, Julia assured me, all went well. It started to fall apart when she'd had to diversify her talents into running the business side and still sell the damn things too.

'I took on too much really,' she admitted. 'But Simone bailed me out, or will do if the deal comes off.' She paused, I only nodded, my decision hadn't yet been made. 'Well, we spent a lot of time together.' This was the bit I wanted to hear, the technicalities were beyond me. 'And I knew she was a dyke and from business to bed was a fairly easy step.'

'I can imagine, knowing you,' I said.

There was a lull in the conversation and yet there was so much I wanted to know. Not just the lurid details, though secondhand sex is better than no sex at all, but Julia could be very evasive about her true feelings sometimes, and my natural curiosity made me want to know more about her and Simone.

Suddenly the woman herself appeared. Julia beamed at the cool woman by our side. I hate to harp on about outfits, but Simone's Yamamoto original would have cost me two years' income at today's egg prices.

Eyes turned to the gorgeous couple and the whole place seemed to take a breath. Classy, classy broads. Simone ordered champagne. 'Moët if you've got it, Cath. Coffee for me.'

The world jumped at her command. Us lesser mortals had to make do with the more mundane, queueing for example.

We swanned over to our table, Simone very much in control as Julia carried the drinks and I trailed behind. I hate playing second fiddle, but third position is even worse. Anne was sitting alone, looking a trifle dazed as Simone commandeered the seat opposite her. Introductions were made and I sat back to watch the two Ms Charmings work their magic. I waited for Caroline to make a reappearance, presuming she'd gone to the loo

48

until Anne explained she'd gone to her room, apparently she suffered migraines. 'Shame,' I said but Simone's wry observations and dry wit entertained us all. Her experience with people was very much in evidence, she skilfully drew Anne out of her shell and I was forced to question my own cynicism, though the warning voice in the back of my mind never quite disappeared.

It was almost one when Simone and Julia took their leave with promises of phone calls, and rather than get thrown out, Anne and I retired to our respective rooms, happily merry and high on the evening.

'Tell Caroline I hope she feels better soon, won't you and thank her again for me.'

Reluctantly I left them to the night ahead, that odd feeling of envy still nagging at me. But envious of what, or whom, I could only guess.

Chapter 7

Breakfast was taken in the bar that only the night before had provided entertainment, magically transformed by the efficient staff.

We were all recovering, to some extent or other, from the effects of the previous night's excesses. The general consensus was that we'd had a great night and would repeat it soon. Anne not surprisingly had been thrilled with the evening, though to my surprise was rather cautious in her assessment of Simone.

'She was a bit too charming for me,' she confessed. 'But I think I could get used to this life,' she added, laughing. It was obvious she was fast embracing, and enjoying, gay culture.

They decided to stay in town for the day, Caroline's migraine had cleared up, and they would return home by train. 'I've got a few purchases I want to make,' Anne said mysteriously. I refused to be drawn, she would doubtless tell me in her own good time.

'Look, why don't you both come for dinner tomorrow? Bring AnnaMaria and what's his name along too if you want.'

Anne, after a moment's guilt at not following her customary routine of dining with Mum, agreed. Caroline declined. 'Other commitments,' she explained. She, too, could be mysterious.

I left Caroline with Simone's folder and bade them both farewell and, after a second's hesitation, kissed Anne on her cheek. She smiled broadly, and I could tell she was touched.

Retrieving my overnight bag, I skipped downstairs, settled my bill and set off for home in my dusty and trusty Land Rover. Melissa accompanied me home and we sang for lost loves and lovers to be. I felt strangely and pleasantly elated and on that journey my decision to accept the car deal, subject to Caroline's report, was made.

I roared into my drive an hour or so later and was momentarily dismayed to find my front door wide open. Relief flooded me as Erik shot out chased by a sunburnt and oily mechanic. AnnaMaria's boyfriend waved to me as he thundered past. Waving back, I parked up. AnnaMaria emerged from the house, intent upon some strange gadget she was madly polishing.

'Do you want the good news first or the bad news?' she said brightly.

'Neither,' I said. 'I just want a cup of tea. Would you like one?' She turned on her heel and followed me into the house.

'Well, the good news is the car's nearly fixed,' she said, ignoring my comment. 'And the bad news is, well there's two really. One, it'll cost you three hundred for parts, and two, Erik's been in your bedroom.'

'Oh Christ,' I said. 'He's getting his own back for me turfing him out of the barn.' I sighed. 'What parts need replacing?'

'Andy's found a wrecked 2CV at the scrap yard, so we got lots of bits from that, but mainly just a new roof and an exhaust really. It's knackered, makes a hell of a noise and they're a bugger to find for your model nowadays but we found one in Huddersfield. It should be ready for collection on Monday, is that okay?'

Thinking quickly I calculated that I had enough in my current account to cover it. It didn't occur to me that I could have simply said no. I was caught up in her enthusiasm.

'Yes, that'll be all right,' I decided and searched in the cupboard for mugs for tea. 'You don't have to go to so much trouble you know. I didn't think Miranda would ever run again.'

AnnaMaria laughed. 'Is that what she's called, Miranda?'

I smiled, remembering. 'Yes, after Carmen Miranda, she always seemed so – exotic somehow.'

'Who?' AnnaMaria asked.

I explained but she looked blank when I mentioned banana headgear. I took the tea to the table, but before we could drink there was a roar from the yard. I shot to the window to see Andy, pleased as punch, waving from the driving seat of my growling 2CV. She made a hell of a racket but she was running, of that there was no doubt.

I hugged AnnaMaria, thrilled despite my reservations and she hugged me back, pleased that her hard work had paid off.

'Come on,' I said, 'I'll drive us round the farm.'

We ran out like a couple of schoolgirls, persuaded a smiling Andy to get in the back and we were off, farting and backfiring down the dirt track that ran through my property. I grappled at first with the dashboard gear change, but soon got the hang of it again.

The brakes were fine, if a little unusual after the gas-powered ones of my Land Rover; I'd had them replaced shortly before she'd stopped running, and she cruised happily, if noisily at thirty miles an hour. After tootling about for twenty minutes we arrived back at the house, windswept and thrilled.

We talked cars over tea and I told them about plans for the auction. They couldn't have been more thrilled if all profits had been going to them, talking of which, it was time to settle my bill. We thrashed out a reasonable deal and I made the cheque out to AnnaMaria. Andy was unfazed.

'We'll get the exhaust on Monday,' I said. 'It should fit in the Land Rover and I can arrange for an MOT while I'm there.' I was reminded of the feelings I'd had when I'd first purchased the Citroën. The experience is quite unique.

After they left I carefully drove Miranda into the barn, now completely out of bounds to Erik, who glared at me from his vantage point atop the concrete outhouse, home to Cynthia's old but serviceable washing machine. Feeling his eyes on me, I decided to tackle my bedroom. Feathers and shit covered my continental quilt and there was a still warm egg on my dressing table; Erik had obviously invited Henrietta in for a party. The quilt and its smelly cover were shoved into the washer and I'm sure that if Erik could have laughed he would have done. He did the next best thing and crowed instead, for his dinner.

After a quick shower I did a check of the garden. Its size was just about manageable with occasional help, and I picked the fruit of my various crops. I planned on making a hearty vegetable curry for my guests the following day and I stored what I wouldn't need in the barn; Mrs Buckham would sell the produce for me. It was surprising how much business she did. The moneyed lot that lived nearby had land a plenty but it was generally home to exotic shrubs and bushes that looked pretty but were indigestible.

My crops would never make me a living, not unless I used the land that lay fallow at the moment, but Cynthia's careful life-long investments ensured I didn't have to flog myself to a standstill to exist.

I wondered, as I tidied the house, what she would have thought of the auction, but supposed I would never know. Mum would be annoyed to miss it, but she was sunning herself on an extended holiday in San Francisco with her gay brother, my Uncle George. He'd been in the navy for thirty years and he'd decided to retire in the gay city of the Universe. What with a lesbian daughter and a gay brother, it's not surprising Mum thought homosexuality ran in the family.

As nightfall arrived I decided to ring Julia to tell her my decision 'with reservations'. She wasn't in but I left a message; there was one woman that would breathe a sigh of relief today.

'Whatdya think of Caroline then?' AnnaMaria asked me the following day through a mouthful of dry fried potatoes. We were alone, as she'd tactfully waited for her aunt to go to the loo (she'd only had a glass of wine, she either had a bladder the size of a pea or my curry didn't agree with her).

'We clashed a bit,' I admitted eating my lunch at a more sedate pace.

'Huh,' she replied, pausing to drink a glass of water. She'd declined the wine, said it gave her wind. Tact obviously didn't extend to all areas of her life. 'I can't stand her. She's such a know-all. Can I have some more potatoes, please?' she concluded, trying to scrape the pattern off her plate.

'Course you can,' I said, pushing the bowl nearer. I

watched in fascination as a pound of King Edwards disappeared down her throat. She must have only weighed eight stone, I didn't know where she put it.

'Why do you say that anyway, about Caroline?'

'Well, look at her,' she said waving her fork angrily in the air. 'She's got Auntie Anne dangling on a string. She's even thinking of getting a mobile phone so she doesn't miss her calls.' She scoffed at the thought.

'Anne seems to be happy though,' I said, trying for the middle ground.

'You don't see her as much as I do, moping about, waiting for Her Royal Highness to turn up.' She resumed eating as Anne came back into the room.

'Sorry about that,' Anne said. 'I started my period this morning, I've got terrible water retention.'

It's odd, but only a week ago I wouldn't have dreamed we'd have such a conversation.

'Are you seeing Caroline tonight?' I asked Anne innocently.

' 'Fraid not,' she said. 'She's meeting that woman from work tonight about the auction thing.'

I smiled guiltily. 'I hope I haven't ruined any plans.'

'Oh no,' she rejoined. 'We don't usually see each other on a Sunday.' She looked thoughtful as she tackled a sparrow's portion of curry.

We ate in silence for a while and AnnaMaria, ditching any attempts at tact, suddenly exploded, 'Look, Auntie, I don't know why you bother with her.'

We both looked up in surprise.

'I thought you approved,' Anne said, only slightly less embarrassed than me at AnnaMaria's remark.

'Oh, I do, about you being a dyke,' she continued. Anne coloured slightly. 'I just don't like her, you could do better you know.' She looked at me pointedly and I pretended not to get the message.

'It takes all sorts,' I clichéd uncomfortably.

'Well, I don't like the way she treats her.' Anna-Maria's cards were firmly on the table. It was down to Anne to challenge her, not me.

Anne sat back and pushed her plate away, clearly upset. 'I know,' she said simply, and a tear slid to the end of her nose.

God, my dinner party was turning into the disaster of the decade. I left my seat and slipped my arm around the woman. My womb did a little song and dance as she rested her head on my breast, but I pushed my sudden lust down. I was surprised at the unexpected rush of feeling, it was unworthy of Anne and I refused to be as tactless as her niece.

'Stick the kettle on, love,' I said to AnnaMaria and drew Anne to the settee positioned in front of the kitchen's gas fire. I sat beside her, stroking her hands, refusing to accept that I wanted to be stroking something else entirely. Her tears slowly abated,

'I'm sorry,' Anne said. 'It's just been so difficult since Saturday.'

'Why, what happened?' I asked, appalled at my friend's distress. 'I thought everything was going so well.'

'It was,' she assured me. 'I feel so . . . rejected.' She looked utterly miserable. 'One minute everything was fine and then Saturday it all fell apart.' AnnaMaria brought tea as Anne got herself under control.

'We went for a drink in the pub just up from the hotel, the one with the pool tables.' I nodded, I knew the place, a hotbed of youngsters playing 'pass the partner'. I know, I'd done it myself.

'And of course there were women there she knew. One in particular she knew from Leeds let something slip, deliberately I think, and, and . . .' She fought the

56

sobs that threatened. I attempted to soothe her but I was at a loss. Tears streamed down her face and I hugged her again.

'She's seeing this other woman as well,' she said bitterly. She hid her face in her hands and gently I prised them away.

'Oh, Anne, I'm so sorry. I'll help if I can.'

'I know, Letty, and thanks, but I'll have to sort it out myself. I can't believe I've been so stupid. And the worst thing is, the worst thing . . .' Anne's sobs were heartbreaking, 'is that I've met her. She introduced us a couple of weeks ago. Can you believe it? I think she's called Jackie or Josie or something, some office worker type,' she added meaninglessly. 'We'd never mentioned monogamy, I just took it for granted. I feel such a fool.'

Oh God, that old stumbling block. I tried not to dwell on my own misdeeds of the past.

'But I told her,' she said sitting up, 'I told her she's got to make a choice, I'm too old to be treated like an idiot.' Her stiff upper lip stiffened noticeably.

AnnaMaria clattered about with tea cups as Anne paused for thought. 'Have you got anything stronger?' she asked. I looked at AnnaMaria's dishwater tea and decided she was being diplomatic.

'Not wine,' Anne added. 'I'll never drink it again, it would just remind me of her.' Venom punctuated her words.

'Would you have her back?' I pried delicately as I pressed a glass of brandy into her hand.

'Oh, I don't know,' she wailed. 'I've never had feelings like that about anyone. She seemed so fond of me, so genuine, it's like a huge betrayal somehow. She never gave me a choice. Never said, how do you feel about monogamy. I can't bear to think of her hopping from someone else's bed into my own. You probably just think I'm an infatuated old fool with no experience. Well, maybe not with women,' she faltered and took a drink, 'but I've had plenty of life experience, ask her,' she said indicating AnnaMaria.

Her niece nodded enthusiastically. 'She's had to put up with me for one thing,' she said deprecatingly. 'For nearly seventeen years,' she added. The message hit me in the face.

'Birthday coming up by any chance?' I asked.

She grinned. 'Next week.'

Our exchange had given Anne a moment to recover. 'What will you do now?' I asked her.

'I know what I'd do,' AnnaMaria mumbled.

'Caroline said she'd ring me. I'll have to see how I feel then. I'm sorry for ruining your meal,' she added.

'You didn't ruin mine,' AnnaMaria chortled. 'When she rings, tell her to get stuffed.'

I was inclined to go along with that suggestion and I was beginning to quite admire Anne's niece.

'I feel better already,' Anne said. 'Just to talk about it helps. You've been really lovely with me, Letty.' She squeezed my hand and smiled at me. I suddenly wanted to fight dragons for her. Instead I plied her with more brandy.

'So what are your plans for your birthday?' I turned to AnnaMaria.

Her enthusiasm knew no bounds. 'A party!' she exclaimed. 'Anne's throwing me a party!' She rubbed her hands together with glee. 'You can come too, if you want.'

Images of seventeen-year-olds off their heads on cider (or whatever) prevailed. I was about to shake my head but Anne said, 'Please come, if only to keep me company.'

How could I refuse?

'Will Andy be going too?' I asked AnnaMaria politely.

'If he plays his cards right,' she said. 'I sometimes wish I fancied women,' she added thoughtfully. Anne's sharp intake of breath was the only sign of her surprise. 'Men are such pillocks, but I can't help liking their bods.'

Her honesty was no mean thing.

'Talking of which,' she said, 'Andy's picking me up in ten minutes.'

'I'd better be going, too,' Anne said.

I couldn't help myself. 'Do you have to rush off?'

'Not really, it's half-day closing tomorrow.'

I grinned like a fool. 'Stay awhile then,' I said. 'I've got this brilliant video.'

At 'video' AnnaMaria's ears pricked up, but promises of a night of passion with Andy prevailed.

'What is it?' Anne asked intrigued. I'd got the impression she was a movie buff on Friday's shopping expedition. She'd exclaimed over the Mel Brooks selection in Smith's as we'd passed by. That's probably why I'd nipped in and bought *The Producers* on my way home. She was impressed as, unbeknown to me at the time, had been the intention.

AnnaMaria departed at the sound of Andy's motorbike and we were left to drink and chuckle all the way through Mel's magical mystery tour. It was as fresh as the first time around and Anne was an instant fan. The brandy, Courvoisier, not just any old shit, went from full to a third in several easy stages.

Too soon it was time for her to leave. I made coffee, an inadequate effort at sobriety, and when I brought it back into the lounge Anne was deep in dreamland, sprawled across the settee. She had temporarily left this mortal coil and my attempts to revive her proved fruitless. I pulled off her shoes, new tan boots I noticed, resisted the temptation to remove any more of her clothes and left her warm, cosy and drunk in front of a low burning fire. My spare quilt added to her sense of comfort and I reluctantly left her to sleep.

Once in bed, after drinking both my coffee and her own, I had a chance to think seriously about my unexpected feelings. And they were unexpected, though I very much doubted if they would ever be reciprocated. The pain she felt at Caroline's behaviour was evident on her face, even in sleep.

Troubled, yet excited, I counted chickens till dawn.

Anne groaned a greeting as I breezed past her to keep said chickens happy. Fortunately brandy, especially a good one, doesn't seem to have any adverse effects on me. Anne wasn't one of those lucky souls and she craved tea, aspirin and an hour's complete silence. With a determination to thwart my newly developing feelings these three requests were easy to fulfil.

I shooed the chickens onto the bottom field where they could eat and squawk merrily all day should they wish and I happily gathered eggs from their open-plan home.

The first omelette was almost ready when Anne staggered into the kitchen. At some point in the night she'd stripped to her knickers and vest and the sight of her firm and muscular legs had my newfound intentions threatening to collapse at the first hurdle.

She lowered herself delicately into a chair. 'I've been thinking,' she said as I placed her breakfast in front of her. 'About Caroline.'

'Oh yes,' I said as I took a place opposite.

'I'm going to ring her,' she paused. 'Today.'

'And tell her what?' I asked. 'To get stuffed?' and smiled, remembering AnnaMaria's ferocity.

'Yes, actually. But perhaps not in so many words.'

'Brave of you,' I said admiringly.

'Not really. I'd rather end it in the early days than wait for it to . . .'

I patted her hand (there was an awful lot of it going on) and shifted her untouched plate. She didn't have to explain, I'd been through it all myself.

She went to the lounge to finish dressing and left a short while later. I was left alone to wait, and hope, a little.

Chapter 8

Several things happened that week that changed my life. For one, Miranda my darling car, sailed through her MOT prompting a new era in our lives. Secondly, I received a rather frosty report from Caroline confirming the feasibility of the car auction.

The third event? All will be revealed later.

Julia rang me to thank me for giving the green light to her project. She tried to explain the intricacies of the event but I cut her short.

'Look, forget the technicalities. Just do whatever it is you've got to do and let me know the exact date you've set for it.'

Before she rang off she made a proposition. 'Just a sec,' she said. 'We begin advertising next week and I thought the best way to give it a kick start would be to throw a dinner dance. It's worked in the past, you know, buttering up all the right people.'

I didn't know but I took her word for it. 'So?' I said.

'What do you mean "so"? The auction's being held on your land, right?'

'Right.'

'Therefore as gracious loaner of land . . .'

'Until the money comes in.'

'Yes, of course, until the money comes in. Anyway never mind all that. I'd like you to come to the Ball, Cinders.'

'Give over, Julia. Can you imagine me there? All those silly bastards, fat gits in tuxedos and dicky bows. I don't think so.'

'Yes, and that's just the women!' Julia howled with laughter down the phone. 'I'm serious,' she said after a moment. 'It's women only.'

'How many rich women do you know, for God's sake?'

'You'd be surprised,' she said chuckling again at her own joke. 'This is a private function anyway. There'll be a separate one for all the hetty big wigs later on. Come on, Letty, you'll love it. Invite Anne and dreadlocks if you want.'

'They've finished,' I said bluntly.

'Already?' Julia squeaked. 'I thought it was all new to Anne.'

'It was, but she's a fast learner. Caught dear dreadlocks with her trousers down, fumbling with someone else.'

'Literally?' Julia gasped.

'Please,' I said. 'Not everyone's like you.'

'Ouch,' Julia said and laughed gently, for I had indeed caught Julia *in flagrante delicto* during our relationship. Ancient but memorable history which Julia will always feel uncomfortable about. There was a moment's silence.

'Are you coming then, or what?'

I could invite Anne. 'Go on then, put me down for two tickets.'

'And who will you be inviting? Let me guess, Anne!'

'Yes.' I sighed and had a sudden inspirational thought. 'Put me down for three tickets instead.'

63

'*Menage à trois* now?' Julia giggled.

'No,' I said. 'I'll leave the seventeen-year-old to you.'

Julia laughed, ignoring my dig. 'Oh, ho. The mad niece. I remember her. Like a female James Dean. Though just remember, Letty, formal attire only. If she turns up in a leather jacket, she won't get in.'

'Julia, you are such a fucking snob. Just what sort of tossers are you knocking about with?'

'Letty!' She feigned shock. 'They're my friends you're talking about. Such opinions and you've not even met them!'

'Your friends?' I asked. 'Or Simone's?'

She chuckled 'Yes, yes, yes. You've caught me out. They are her friends and most of them are tossers. But they're tossers with money and connections. They won't do the business any harm.'

'I'm sorry,' I said contritely. 'It's nothing to do with me.'

'Hey, Letty,' Julia said, concern in her voice. 'What's wrong, love?'

'Another time,' I said, loath to share intimate feelings over the phone.

'That's twice you've fobbed me off lately,' Julia scolded. 'Well, you know where I am if you need me. I'll send you your tickets today, we've hired a function room at the Town Hall, no expense spared, you know.'

'If I didn't know better, I'd swear you were one of Thatcher's children.'

'Blasphemy!' Julia exploded. 'You know I'm a member of New Labour.'

'You are the most unlikely socialist I've ever met.' I giggled, my mood suddenly lifting.

'Well, I'm in good company then, aren't I? No time for politics now. Business calls. Look forward to seeing you Monday. Don't be late. 7.30 sharp. Bye.'

And she was gone.

However, before I temporarily joined the lezzy jet set, I had a more normal and probably more enjoyable function to attend; AnnaMaria's seventeenth birthday party.

When I got to Anne's home the following Thursday evening, reluctantly sacrificing *Eastenders* (Anne assured me later I would get my reward in heaven) for, I assumed, an apocalyptic drinking bout, I hardly recognised the woman that answered the door.

AnnaMaria had left her Acid Jazz Freak outfit in the wardrobe and appeared at the door in a simple black frock. She looked gorgeous, but I was vaguely disappointed; I'd got to quite like her eccentric apparel. There was a partial reprieve in that she'd shaved off most of her hair and what was left was dyed a wicked blonde.

AnnaMaria whipped my carrier bag from my hands and the bottles clinked together precariously. Peering in, she exclaimed a simple 'wow' and disappeared down the hall toward the kitchen. I let myself in and shut the door behind me, gradually getting my breath. I'd been in a state all evening. What should I wear (what would Anne like me in)? What should I take to drink (would Anne like brandy again)? Blah, blah, blah.

I had gone for safety, jeans and T-shirt and I brought the brandy. The beer was for everyone under eighteen, and me. Following AnnaMaria's footsteps into the kitchen I discovered Anne up to the eyeballs in food preparation. She beamed when she saw me, her already flushed cheeks going pinker still.

'Hiya,' she said. I smiled in return, every atom delighted to see her. 'Grab a knife and get slicing,' she ordered, and pushed a bag of tomatoes across the work surface. Her bright white kitchen groaned with food.

'Feeding of the five thousand, is it?' I asked as I took a place beside her.

'Most of her friends turned up,' she said. 'All of them with seventeen-year-old appetites. I thought food might dilute the effects of the beer a bit, I don't want them throwing up everywhere.'

AnnaMaria busily uncorking a bottle of wine, butted in. 'If they throw up, I'll throw them out,' she promised. 'I'm the one that cleans the house, after all.' She disappeared through the door that led to the lounge. Rave music got louder as the door swung open and faded to a dull thud as it closed behind her.

'Don't ask,' Anne said pre-empting my words. 'She's not only turned over a new leaf, but the whole bloody tree.'

I laughed. 'What's she studying then?' I said, madly slicing tomatoes.

'She wants to be a mechanic,' Anne replied, smiling, obviously proud of her niece's new venture. Anne took the tomatoes from me and threw them willy nilly on to various sandwiches.

'That's it, if they want anything else, they'll have to go to the chippy. Give them a shout, would you?'

I stuck my head through the door. Andy was nearby deep in thought over an album cover.

'Grub's ready,' I yelled at him over the din. He gave me the thumbs up, he was a man of few words.

Anne was pouring brandy when I returned. She'd taken her pinny off and she looked lovely.

'You look gorgeous,' I said before I could stop myself.

'Thank you,' she said smiling. 'You look pretty good yourself.'

Did I? Ordinary was the word I would have used.

Her clothes, a grey calf-length skirt and black long-sleeved T-shirt, were well cut and accentuated her rather curvaceous figure. She handed me a glass and led me to the front room, out of bounds to the revellers. There was something to be said for the old three-roomed terraces.

'How're things?' I ventured. I'd not seen her since the day of the meal and she'd not been in touch. It had been all I could do not to ring her.

She sat on the couch and gestured for me to join her. 'Not as bad as I thought they'd be,' she said, choosing her words carefully.

'You ended it then?'

'Oh yes,' Anne said. 'Caroline told me she had no intention of finishing with the other woman.'

'Charming,' I said, and took a slug of the brandy, mainly to stop my hands shaking. Anne was having a very odd effect on me. She got up from the settee and stood with her back to the open fire. There was a moment's awkward silence. I couldn't figure out why.

'What's wrong?' I asked. 'Are you still upset?'

'Well, yes,' she replied, gazing at her drink. 'But not about Caroline.' She didn't look at me and my heart did slow, lazy somersaults in my chest.

'What then?' I stammered.

'I thought you might have rung,' she said finally.

I got to my feet and stood with her by the fire. 'I was hoping you'd ring me,' I said. 'I didn't want to interfere.'

She smiled, and tension drained away. That small moment when I could have comfortably gone to her and held her passed too swiftly.

'What happened?' I asked, grabbing the mantelpiece instead for support.

'Well, it was odd really,' Anne said, eyes distant with the memory. 'I rang her on Monday afternoon, I knew she was off that day, and another woman answered. There was some whispered conversation, I could hear them in the background. And then Caroline came on the phone, all giggly and daft, not like her at all, she's usually quite a serious sort of person. Anyway, I told her what I felt.'

'And?' I prompted.

'And nothing. For all the effect it had on her I might as well have asked her to get a pizza on the way home.'

I stifled a smile at the odd comparison. It was obvious Anne was angry, humiliated even, but not upset in an emotional way. 'So what did you do?'

AnnaMaria stuck her head round the door at that moment. 'She took my advice,' she said, 'and told her to fuck off.'

'And good riddance, too,' Anne said decisively. She raised her glass and toasted us both.

The party was a hit, as predicted, and no one was sick, except the cat, who ate too much.

I stayed overnight in the spare room, desperately wishing that the wall that separated us would fall down.

It didn't.

AnnaMaria, who had decided to tidy the house as the last guest left, paid me a call. She was still a bit the worse for wear, not surprising considering the amount of beer she'd put away. She clutched a battered cheese sandwich in her hand as she took a seat on the edge of the bed.

'Are you awake?' she asked, prodding me through the quilt. I peeked over the cover and queasily watched her devour her food.

'I've brought you some tea,' she said.

'What time is it?' I mumbled, loath to acknowledge her.

'About five,' AnnaMaria replied through a mouthful

of bread. Crumbs cascaded onto the bedcover. She waited for me to surface. Protest was pointless, so I sat up and took a drink from the mug proffered. It was still dishwater laced with milk; she hadn't quite got the hang of it yet.

'Did you enjoy yourself?' I managed after a couple of swallows. The room swam out of focus a few times but I made an effort to fight the effect.

'Brilliant!' she said. 'Fucking brilliant. Anne's a real star, you know? All that for me,' she paused. 'And you.'

'What?' I asked. I was too knackered for riddles.

'Come on, Letty,' AnnaMaria said. She peered at me, an incredulous look on her face. 'You must have noticed.'

I hadn't noticed anything, except the fast-emptying brandy bottle, oh, and the beer, which was why I felt like shit.

'I saw you disappear into the garden,' she said triumphantly.

'She was just asking me if I'd help her clear the plot,' I protested. Memories flooded back.

'Yeah, yeah,' she scorned.

'Honestly,' I said, though I didn't know why I was justifying myself.

'I can't believe you two!' AnnaMaria shot back. 'It's obvious you fancy each other, what are you waiting for, the full moon?' She laughed at her own odd joke, leaned over, kissed me on the cheek again and swanned out.

'Oh,' she paused at the door, 'thanks for my present, it was dead sweet of you.'

'You're welcome,' I called to her departing back. I'd booked five driving lessons with the local instructor. With her past record that was probably all she'd need for her test. I know it sounds extravagant but she'd done me enough favours.

I settled back for another kip and to savour what AnnaMaria had said. Had there been words in the house or was she simply an astute teenager? Was I so obvious and did Anne feel the same?

A surge of happiness hit me as I tumbled into sleep. I dreamt of long grey skirts and warm and wanting flesh.

Emerging at ten I stumbled downstairs. The house was spotless and smelt of coffee. AnnaMaria, with enough energy for ten, was madly buttering round after round of toast. She dumped some in front of me.

'What about the chickens?' she demanded. Vegetarian and animal-rights protester, she didn't want me shirking my duties.

'George from next door promised to see to them.' Honestly, Erik and his brood ran my life. 'I'll have to go soon though,' I said, a trifle guiltily. 'I've got a few things to do. Oh, by the way do you think you can make it to a dinner dance on Monday at the Town Hall, in Manchester, that is. Women only, some advertising thing Julia's cooked up. Best bib-and-tucker apparently,' I added innocently.

Her eyes narrowed. 'Frightened I'd turn up in leather, was she?'

I ignored her comment. 'Ask Anne too, of course. I told her last night but she's probably forgotten.'

'No, I haven't forgotten,' Anne said from the kitchen door. She reached for some toast and squeezed my shoulder as she edged past me. I nearly choked.

'Morning,' she smiled, eyes twinkling. I twinkled back.

They both agreed to accompany me the following Monday, which brightened my day no end.

I was tempted to dally awhile, but I knew I had things to do, so I said my goodbyes and meandered home.

Chapter 9

A catalogue lay on my doorstep as I arrived home. It was expensive, glossy and impressive, as were the cars pictured. I was amazed at the range and over a coffee I examined the inventory. There were several truly rare models, imported from all over the world. A pre-war Mercedes Speedster 400 had been found in Colombia and a few paragraphs told its remarkable history.

It was believed to have been shipped over from Germany in 1944, along with its high-flying owner Colonel Hopmann, an officer in the Waffen SS who had decided to do a bunk when the war took a downward turn for Germany. Not wanting to leave his home comforts behind, he'd carted his car and his kids (there was no mention of wifey) to the city of Medellin, where the car had been stored and forgotten until its discovery by the Colonel's granddaughter Leisel, in 1989. Rebuilt and now in pristine condition it was worth an estimated £70,000.

Seventy thousand pounds! Fuck me, I hoped their insurance was up to date. Stunned, I took a drink of my now cold coffee and counted the number of cars to be auctioned. Thirty-five, the Merc being the most expensive. Even an Austin A30 was expected to fetch a couple of grand. We were talking big, big, money here. I felt a twinge of anxiety about the proceedings. But, what the hell, it wasn't my problem. Even if it was the world's biggest flop it wouldn't do me any harm, I'd either make money or I wouldn't. Selfish, I know, but these people were in a different league to me, even Julia would bounce back, whatever happened, and my one per cent commission was looking increasingly attractive.

I skipped through the rest of the catalogue and noted that a date had been set for the second week of October, in almost three weeks' time.

A covering note was attached from Simone.

'I hope these days suit,' she'd written.

If not let me know as soon as possible. The shipping schedules are a bit tight I'm afraid, and I'd so hate for the star attraction to miss the show.

It took me a moment to realise that she meant the Hopmanns' Mercedes.

Leisel Hopmann, the owner, is coming to England too. Chances are you will meet her on Monday. Please let me know about the dates. I look forward to meeting you again.

She signed it simply 'Simone'.

I decided to ring Simone's office to confirm the dates and of course she wasn't in and I was forced to deal with Jocelyn the Repugnant Receptionist. She put me on hold for five minutes, I'm sure just to try my patience, and when she came back on the line she was finishing a conversation with someone whose voice sounded vaguely familiar.

'. . . October,' I heard Jocelyn say angrily. 'The deal's set for then.'

'I don't give a fuck,' the voice answered. 'I've done my bit. I want some money up front now.'

'You'll have to speak to Steigel yourself,' Jocelyn snapped back. The door to the office was suddenly slammed shut, the noise carrying only too well over the phone.

My memory cleared and I recognised the other woman's voice. Caroline. Odd that she should be at Simone's, though perhaps not so strange what with all the networking that went on in lesbian money circles nowadays. I wondered, briefly, what sort of deal she was involved in and made myself a mental note to ask Julia, but then I found myself in verbal combat with Jocelyn and the thought was banished under the assault.

It wasn't until the following week that I had cause to comment on the conversation I'd overheard.

I rang Anne every day prior to the dinner dance. She rang me too, sometimes for the most transparent of reasons. Books were a good one. She must have searched the bowels of Library HQ to come up with some of the titles. AnnaMaria was a common denominator too. We agreed that in the last few weeks she'd calmed down considerably. Anne thought that college may have been good for her, but I suspected that it was Anne herself that had the influence. She resisted the idea, hardly imagining herself as a good foster mother.

'Better to be a friend,' I suggested. She was silent, unwilling to accept that wild AnnaMaria may have just turned into a success story.

I ended each conversation reluctantly. We were

discovering each other in the gentlest of ways, while I tried not to think of my soaring phone bills.

Sunday was a pig of a day. I'd decided to cut my hair and it all went disastrously wrong. I couldn't even bear to look at myself in the mirror. I was on the point of shaving the lot off despite not having the looks of Sinead to carry it off, when an unexpected visitor stopped the scalping.

'Julia,' I said stupidly, still clutching the clippers.

'What in God's name have you done to your hair?' she demanded. She snatched the clippers from my hand and guided me into a kitchen chair.

'What's with you and this cost-cutting shit?' she mumbled as she examined the disaster area. 'You were less frugal when you had nothing, and don't give me this feud with the local hairdresser excuse. You were in town last weekend, why didn't you get it cut then? Even Anne managed that.'

I didn't bother with an answer, she would never understand my motives. Why should she? I didn't.

'Right,' she continued. 'You've got two choices. Either let me do something with it, or I'll treat you to Vidal's.'

'Not a bad offer from someone with no money,' I retorted. 'Anyway, you know that they intimidate me. Personal choice goes out the window the minute you walk through the door.' I shuddered at the memory of past expenditure.

'Looks like it's me then,' she said and snapped on the clippers.

Half-an-hour later, after much snipping, combing and gelling, I was left with a quite presentable flat top.

'Well, Ms Rossi,' I said, finally able to look at my reflection. 'And which girly taught you these tricks?'

She grinned into the mirror. 'I just happen to have very talented fingers,' she said.

I resisted a rather obvious and tacky reply but smirked as an unbidden memory flooded my mind. Something to do with a wild afternoon spent with her on the moors in the back of her company car. And we weren't having a picnic.

'Stick the kettle on,' Julia demanded. 'Nowadays I'll accept a cuppa in exchange for my abilities.'

'That's all I'm offering,' I said, laughing.

'Letty, my love, you've not changed one bit, have you? It always narked me that yours was the quicker wit.'

'Years of practising on you,' I quipped.

'You see,' she said. 'That's just what I mean!'

Laughing together, the barriers tumbled and we were friends again.

'Is this a social visit then, or what?' I asked as we sat nursing mugs of tea.

'Social and business really,' Julia said seriously. She ran her fingers through her dark hair and, exquisitely cut as it was, it immediately fell back into place. Sighing deeply, she rested her chin in her hand. Suddenly she looked tired and drained, as though everything was a bit of an effort.

I reached across the table and rubbed the tanned skin of her forearm. I'd not seen her quite so sad for a long time.

'Trouble?' I asked gently. Julia nodded. She looked as miserable as a Sumo wrestler that had been told to go on a diet.

'Money?' I probed.

'If only that were all,' she mumbled.

'Simone then?' The words blood and stone sprang to mind. However I took her grunted reply as an affirmative. My powers as an agony aunt were about to be tested again. I felt like ringing AnnaMaria; she was much better at it than me.

'Let's go for a walk,' I suggested. I looked her up and down. 'Though you're not really dressed for it.'

Her hand-made Italian shoes, probably sent over by her Mafiosi grandfather, were lovely but wouldn't last five minutes on the farm.

'I've got some wellies that might fit.' A haughty look from her lovely grey eyes told me where I could shove that suggestion.

'I thought your car was fixed,' she said. 'Can't we go for a drive instead?'

Not known for her fitness regime, Julia was the type of person who, if she could, would gladly hire someone to painlessly exercise her body.

'Okay,' I sighed. 'But I don't think there's much petrol in it. We'll drive to the bottom fields, you can give me the low-down on what to expect in October.'

We, well, I, trudged to the barn to get the car out. She started first time, the blue smoke nearly choking me, but at least we were moving.

Picking Julia up from the front door (she was so lazy sometimes it was unbelievable) we chugged down the dirt track to the fields beyond. The weather had started to change and black clouds threatened in the distance. It did nothing to lighten Julia's mood. I clicked my window open and threw back the new roof to let a little light and air on to the proceedings, thinking we'd probably need it.

And I was right.

'It's lovely here, isn't it?' Julia said as we took in the scenery. 'I used to come here and watch the sun go down, it was the best bit about living here.'

'Thanks,' I said suppressing a smile.

'Oh, you know what I mean,' she said.

'Yeah,' I admitted. 'This lot was never your cup of tea really, was it? You were always happiest doing business deals over lunch. I was gobsmacked when you wanted to move here.'

She turned to look at me and smiled, the exhaustion lifting from her face. 'It was you I wanted to be with, you know. Not the farm and certainly not the bloody chickens.'

I grinned back. 'Yes, well at least we gave it a go.'

'And we're still friends,' Julia said.

'Yep, still friends,' I agreed.

We sat in silence for a while enjoying the peace of the countryside.

Finally Julia spoke. 'I don't know what to do, Letty.' She gazed out of the window at the gathering clouds and real pain lay etched on her face. 'About Simone,' she added, almost to herself. She reached up and pressed two fingers against her forehead, as though she could rub her troubles away.

'What's happened?' I asked quietly.

For a second her fingers pressed harder against her skin and she closed her eyes, blotting out some awful reality.

She turned to face me. 'Do you know who the other Steigel is?' she asked.

I must admit I'd had some thoughts on the matter. 'Father?' I guessed.

Julia's smile was a painful thing to see. Her tight, white lips hid an anger I could only guess at. As if on cue a low rumble of thunder sounded in the distance and the first fat drops of rain began to fall. Her grimace faded and she shook her head sadly. She suddenly

clenched her fist and slammed it hard against the dashboard. The steering wheel vibrated with the blow.

She turned to face me. 'It's her husband,' she hissed.
'Her fucking husband!'

I hurriedly replaced the roof as the rain began in
earnest. It gave me time to think.

Julia was oblivious to the rain, unconcerned at any
discomfort and indifferent to her surroundings.

'How married are they?' I tried after a moment's
silence. Julia went back to kneading her forehead.

'She still fucks him if that's what you mean,' she said,
through clenched teeth.

'Oh, God,' I muttered, knowing Julia's thoughts on
such matters. She'd been out with straight women
before, usually with terrible results.

'Did she tell you?' I asked gently.

'What do you think?' she snapped. 'She knows how
I feel about sleeping with women that are still fucking
men. It's emotional disaster. I should know, I've been
on the losing end often enough.'

Julia always imagined she would be successful at con-
version jobs, and usually it was only her pride that got
hammered when she failed. This time it was her heart.

'So how did you find out?' I asked, ignoring her
angry outburst.

'Caroline let it slip,' she replied.

'Caroline?' I spluttered. 'When?'

'I bumped into her at Simone's office the other
day . . .'

'Why was she there?' I interrupted, a hidden memory
prompting the question.

'Oh, some deal she's doing with Simone's firm, I
don't know what exactly. I didn't really like her when
we met, I like her even less now, devious little shit. At

least I remembered where I knew her from. She's been in Simone's office before, I think she knows Jocelyn. They used to work together or something. I don't know,' she mumbled, 'I don't really care, either.'

Anger momentarily overcame heartbreak.

'So what happened?'

Julia took a deep breath. 'It's not easy you know,' she mumbled. She turned her face from me but not before I'd seen her eyes fill with tears. 'I suppose it wasn't really Caroline's fault. We were in the wrong place at the wrong time, or right time, depending how you look at it. It's amazing isn't it? I've been seeing her, loving her,' she paused and swallowed hard, fighting tears, 'trusting her for six months and I never knew. I feel as big a fool as Anne did, but at least her lover was sleeping with another woman.'

I didn't know how that made things better, betrayal is betrayal in my book.

'Did you never ask who the partners were?'

'Of course I did. Blomquest doesn't exist apparently, or so she said. She told me the other Steigel was a family member, a sleeping partner.' She laughed at the irony but there was little humour in the sound. 'I'd had to go to Simone's office to finalise details about the auction. I'd been there an hour, longer than I'd intended but I find it so hard to leave her, you know? I wanted to take her to lunch but she had a prior arrangement, with her fucking husband no doubt.' She spat the word out.

I felt more than a twinge of sympathy for her. First her business and now this.

'As I was leaving, Caroline walked through the door. I was surprised to see her, you can imagine, but Simone does all sorts of business with all sorts of people and lesbian businesswomen tend to attract each other. I was just going to say hello really, but something made me ask.' She paused and fumbled in her pocket for her cigarettes. 'Do you mind?' she asked, shaking the packet.

'No,' I said. 'I'll have one too.'

Julia expressed no surprise, she'd seen me stop and start smoking for years. She lit both cigarettes and the smoke drifted through the open windows into the damp beyond.

'What did you say?' I prompted. She was a sod for losing her line of thought, even in a situation like this.

'Well, I told her that Simone was free. Hell of an assumption, huh? I'm sure Caroline was smirking when she assured me it wasn't Simone she'd come to see. For one mad moment I thought she'd called for Jocelyn the Dragon Lady, but she was out to lunch anyway. "No," she said, "I'm not here to see Simone, I've come to see Richard." I must have looked puzzled, I mean who the hell was Richard? As far as I was aware there was no one in the place except Simone. She brushed past me, you know what she's like, and knocked on the door of what I'd always presumed to be an empty office. She waltzed in before there was a reply and whispered to me, "You know. Richard, Simone's husband." '

Julia flicked her cigarette out the window. 'I don't know why I didn't see Simone about it there and then. You can't believe how I felt. I just stormed out and went back to work. I've not been able to think about anything else since.'

'So you don't really know what the score is then?'

'Oh, I know all right. All those excuses when she couldn't stay over, driving miles out of town for expensive dinners. Never meeting her family, telling me they were all still living in Sweden. Such shit and I fell for it. And then sleeping with me after screwing him. It makes me sick,' she added bitterly.

'Have you said anything to her?' I asked.

'I've not seen her since. I rang her and told her I had too much work on. The truth is I can't face her yet. And to think someone like Caroline knows more about her than I do. God Almighty!'

Angrily she lit another cigarette and blew smoke morosely out of the window.

'You've got to see her, you know,' I said, ditching the butt in the ashtray. The Gauloise had made me feel a bit queasy.

'I know, I know,' she said, slapping the dashboard again. The car would drop to bits at this rate. 'I was hoping to have some sort of future with her.' She shook her head. 'I don't think I can face her yet,' she repeated.

Heartbroken, the tears that had threatened suddenly became real and they rolled wetly down her face. She leaned against me and all the sadness and bitterness she felt was exposed to the world. Well, to me at any rate.

The scene was horribly reminiscent of the one I'd had with Anne. Odd that Caroline had had a hand in both affairs.

'Why don't you ring her?' I suggested. 'You don't have to face her, well not immediately. And then, if you're up to it, you could arrange to meet somewhere on neutral territory, you can have a good slanging match if it would make you feel better. You've got to do something, Julia. There's too much at stake not to.'

She sat up and noisily blew her nose on a spotless hanky she'd produced from her trench coat pocket. 'I could I suppose.' She nodded reluctantly.

'You could invite her here if you want,' I added, impressed with my own ingenuity.

She thought for a moment, teary eyes distant. 'Would you mind?' she asked.

'Oh, for God's sake, of course not. Why don't you ring her now. I can disappear for the afternoon,' and I knew exactly where I'd go, 'but you'll have to feed the chickens later.'

'That's okay,' she sniffed. 'But what will I say to her?'

'Confront her. Tell her what you know. Though let's face it, you don't know that much and what you do know is secondhand from Caroline. Now, would you buy a used car from that woman?'

Julia smiled and shook her head.

'So why do you instantly believe what she says?'

'Why would she lie?' Julia asked, calling my bluff.

'Come on,' I said, having no answer. 'Let's get back while you're still in this frame of mind.'

The car struggled back to the house as the rain turned into a deluge and, sodden, we ran into the kitchen.

A woman dressed in black turned to face us.

Chapter 10

'I'm sorry,' Simone said. 'But the door was open.'

For a few seconds we remained motionless, each waiting for the other to speak. Simone as elegant and beautiful as ever in a suit to die for, cracked first. 'Julia,' she said, 'I've been looking for you.'

'I was going to ring you,' Julia replied, the fire gone from her voice, replaced by a deep sadness.

'You've been crying,' Simone said helplessly and moved toward her. For a moment I thought Julia was going to bolt through the back door. But she remained rooted to the spot as Simone gently wiped her face with her fingers.

I felt intrusive but fascinated as I witnessed this moment of intimacy and hidden passion. 'I'll leave,' I said rather reluctantly, finding my voice at last. Julia looked at me, pleading silently. 'If you want,' I added.

'I can't throw you out of your own house,' Simone turned to me. 'We'll go back to mine.'

'Depends who's waiting there.' Julia's voice chilled me to the bone.

'Please,' I said, 'just get it sorted out. I'm going to Anne's. Julia, if you need me the number's in my phone book.'

I grabbed my car keys and escaped from the oppressive atmosphere. The rain was quite refreshing in comparison.

Driving from my house towards Calderton, I admitted to myself that my reasons for wanting to stay had been less than honourable. But my reasons for wanting to visit Anne were less than honourable too, so I couldn't win either way.

Miranda hiccoughed all the way to the local garage. I was amazed when AnnaMaria came out to serve me.

'I didn't know you were working here,' I said, unscrewing the petrol cap for her.

'New job,' she explained. 'Helps with college.'

I was getting used to seeing her streaked with oil, and today was no exception. Her shaved blonde hair had completely disappeared under a carpet of grease. She carefully filled Miranda with petrol and even wiped off a couple of drops that she'd spilt.

'How's she running?' she asked.

'Well, she'll never make Le Mans,' I quipped, 'but I think she'll get me to your house.'

AnnaMaria grinned. 'She'll be dead chuffed to see you.'

'Good,' I said and grinned along with her as I paid my bill.

The florist near the local cemetery was open and on an impulse I bought a bunch of mixed, out-of-season flowers for Anne and then suddenly feeling foolish, wished I hadn't. I toyed with the idea of putting them on someone's grave but decided that the living would appreciate them more than the dead.

She was waiting on the doorstep as I arrived, arms folded across her chest and a knowing smile across her mouth. Dragging the flowers from the back seat of the car, I saw a number of nets twitch from the row of terraces opposite and gave them a wave to show them that they'd been spotted.

'She rang from the garage then?' I asked as I edged past her into the hall. This close up I could smell her shampoo and I could see the ends of her hair were still damp.

'Who?' she asked innocently, eyes wide.

'Don't "who" me,' I said laughing and handed the flowers over. Her look of pleasure dispelled any discomfort I may have felt.

'Thank you, Letty,' she said and sniffed at the brightly coloured petals. 'They're beautiful,' she added looking directly into my eyes.

'So are you,' I breathed and gently reached to touch her.

Her hand felt dry, warm and welcoming in mine and we stood for an age in that cool, bright hallway, silently acknowledging our growing feelings.

'I'll put these in water, shall I?' And Anne led me into the kitchen.

She hummed to herself as she filled a vase with water and my heart beat double time as I made coffee. For a second we both used the sink at the same time and she briefly laid her head on my arm.

'I knew you'd come today,' she said, voice muffled against my shirt. 'Even before AnnaMaria called.'

'How did you know?' I managed. Her close proximity threatened to overwhelm me.

'Just a feeling.'

Julia turned up in a mess, problems with Simone . . .' I began.

'Tell me later,' Anne interrupted. 'Bring the coffee and come to bed.'

She led me upstairs to her own bedroom as the words began to sink in. Opposing walls of muted greys and soft mulberry accentuated her simple wooden furniture. All except for the bed which was a big, loud brass affair. A bed that shouted, get in, try me for size.

I put the coffee on the dresser by the side of the bed and a not so innocent Anne excited, enticed and seduced me. From the first moment she slipped her hands inside my shirt and caressed my unfettered breasts, I was lost to her. Intense and uncomplicated, her desire was breathtaking and our lovemaking was the same. We were wild together, and gentle together, wet and wanting together. I couldn't resist her and she didn't resist me.

And in the end I was shocked by my need of her, my lust and desire for her. And as I'd hoped, the sensuality and longings were returned.

Later, as come and sweat stickily bound our bodies, we took a moment to catch our breath and reflect on this amazing event.

We lay beneath her bright king-size quilt, toes and fingers touching lightly. I had to keep looking at her, I still couldn't believe we were here together. She leaned on one elbow, chin in hand and gazed back. Her dark hair was in disarray and it fell gently to one side of her forehead. In wonder I ran my hand over the soft spiky hairs at the base of her neck.

'Were you expecting this?' I asked her.

She gently rubbed the space between my breasts before she replied. 'Of course,' she said, biting her bottom lip.

'Oh?' I replied, clutching at her wandering fingers.

She grinned. 'Don't tell me you weren't.'

'I was just hopeful,' I said. Anne's grin turned to laughter and her breath was sweet on my face. She rolled on top of me, pinning me to the bed. 'So what happens now?' she asked. Her full breasts pressed gently against my own and I could barely string a thought together. My hands followed the contours of her full and lovely body.

'Well,' I said. 'Firstly, I want to see you again, secondly, on a monogamous basis and last but not least I'd like to make love to you.'

Anne kissed me, lips swollen and damp with desire. 'Accepted on all three counts,' she said and all shyness gone, she began to explore my body once more.

Of course eventually we had to get out of bed. Anna-Maria was expected at five and I had to get home sooner or later. Later would have been preferable, but the more I put it off the more vivid a picture became of Simone lying across the kitchen floor with a bread knife in her back.

Anne and I had a lingering shower before she pushed me out of the front door homeward bound. AnnaMaria, arriving just as I left the house, immediately spotted the glow around me and recognised its significance, though the only word she said was 'hello'.

My feet were still floating off the floor as I let myself into my kitchen. There were no bodies littered about, dead or otherwise, just a brief note from Julia.

We've gone to Simone's to sort things out. How's Anne?!
Love Julia

I could tell her spirits had lifted. A PS on the reverse of the note ordered, 'Tomorrow. 7.30pm. Town Hall, don't be late.'

I rang Anne before I'd even removed my coat. She answered it on the first ring.

87

'Hiya,' I said grinning like an idiot. I could feel her grin on the other end.

'Any deaths in your neck of the woods?' she asked.

'Surprisingly, no,' I replied. I'd brought her up to date with Simone's chequered past in between bouts of lovemaking.

'You've not forgotten about tomorrow night have you?' I asked her.

'How could I? I just wish it were now,' she added wistfully.

My brief 'just ringing to say hi' phone call lasted an hour and I remembered things I wanted to say to her long after I'd hung up, checked on the animals, made a tea I couldn't eat and finally hit the sack at ten.

To my great delight she rang me ten minutes after my head had hit the pillow, just to wish me the sweetest of dreams. I got up, got in the car and drove back to her house. Neither of us slept a wink.

Chapter 11

I had to leave Anne's bed in the early hours to fulfil my duties as keeper of chickens and Erik was most displeased when his breakfast was an hour late. His female companions sulked and refused to lay an egg that day too. They weren't very happy with the puddles that flooded the yard from the previous day's downpour either, but I couldn't do much about that.

Mithered and distracted, my mind was filled with things other than the routine. Thoughts of Anne accompanied my every task and the temptation to leap up and down was almost overwhelming.

Doubts began to creep in about three o'clock. Would she be happy with me? Were we compatible? Stupidly dwelling on misgivings barely twenty-four hours into the relationship.

I began to consider my own motives. Was I so shallow that a new haircut would turn my head so? The woman had been dropping books off for me for years, what had suddenly made her so attractive? Her newfound assurance?

What? What was it?

The truth dawned after a couple of hours of this pointless rhetoric.

It was obvious. I had always been attracted, always looked forward to her visits, was always eager to know more about her, even if I had to gossip to get information. And suddenly she comes out, has an affair, gains confidence and is suddenly available. The envy I'd suffered the previous weekend had been directed at Caroline. I simply wanted to be in her place.

Recognising this great self-discovery, I was relieved and calmer. I didn't know what sort of relationship Anne and I would have, or how long it was likely to last, none of us can know these things, but I was hopeful.

Was there any wonder that the chickens received extra rations that day?

Anne and her niece met me outside the Post Office at six-thirty. AnnaMaria thought it was hilarious. 'Are you hoping the neighbours won't notice?' she asked.

Though in fact our choice of rendezvous was for far more practical purposes than avoiding gossip. It was a pain in the arse trying to manoeuvre the bulky and noisy Land Rover down Anne's narrow dead-end street. I'd left Miranda in the barn, thinking a trip to and from Manchester might be a bit much for the old girl. AnnaMaria and her boyfriend might have worked wonders but I didn't want to be stranded driving home in the middle of the night.

AnnaMaria didn't swallow the excuse at all. It was plain Anne had told her what had happened between us (the censored version at any rate) and AnnaMaria was obviously hoping she'd be a candidate for chief bridesmaid.

Anne looked lovely as she climbed in beside me and, uncharacteristically, my kiss of welcome was a shy one. My heart did its usual roll of honour. She'd gone to town on her outfit and her grey cotton suit was gorgeous in its simplicity. My suit, a baggy affair I'd had made after my windfall from Aunt Cynthia, still fitted me well, despite the ups and downs (or ins and outs) of my waistline.

AnnaMaria's garment, whatever it was, lay hidden beneath an ageing calf-length parka. All I could see was the bottom half of a pair of black pants and shiny black DM shoes. I only hoped the rest of the outfit was as promising.

I drove to Manchester's Town Hall as Anne's warm and wandering hand played a tune up and down my thigh, under which circumstances I would have driven just about anywhere.

Miraculously I found a parking space near the venue and as we rounded the corner of the Town Hall onto Albert Square we caught the tail end of a group of chattering, expensively dressed women heading up the staircase. Anne raised an eyebrow at me. I knew she was a little reticent about the soirée, hell, so was I. My experience of such sumptuous affairs was limited. Only AnnaMaria seemed unconcerned.

A huge banner hung over the main gates welcoming friends and associates of Classic Cars and announcing the time and place of the forthcoming auction. It was odd to see my address up in lights. I hoped all my future visitors would be welcome ones.

A woman in black and whites collected our coats at the top of the impressive stairway that led to our function room. I needn't have worried about AnnaMaria, she looked absolutely stunning. She would surely be Belle of the Ball and was there any wonder? She's got more than a touch of the chameleon about her. One minute her clothes are so odd she could get a job on Channel 4, then at her own party she wears a dress

Magenta DeVine would kill for and now, well, I think Annie Lennox must have had a car boot sale.

Of course there were ties, suits, dicky bows as well as little black frocks aplenty, but AnnaMaria, understated yet stunning, turned every head. Perhaps they thought she was Ms Lennox, the blonde hair gave her more than a passing resemblance, though I doubted if the singer went out with oil under her fingernails. For me though, her attractiveness was in her damned self-assurance. I wish I'd had an ounce of it when I was seventeen.

The Town Hall, usually a venue devoid of any atmosphere, had been tarted up with no expense spared, courtesy of Simone's firm, judging by the business cards scattered about. The severity of the wood-and-stone structure had been softened by warm, feel friendly fabrics draped elegantly from ceiling to floor. Oriental carpets were littered underfoot, seemingly at random, though I expect an interior designer had spent sleepless nights organising the whole thing.

The effect was stunning and the furnishings, combined with the extraordinary lighting, made me feel as though I were in an overlarge country manor, not one of Manchester's most prestigious buildings. As we entered this amazing scene another woman, whose attire was surely authentic tailored livery of the nineteenth century, proffered champagne on a silver tray. We each took a glass and AnnaMaria knocked hers back with a flourish. 'You'd better make the most of it,' she muttered in an aside, quickly grabbing another glass. 'I bet you have to buy your own after this.'

Cocktail dresses and fancy suits walked by and I knew not a one. Not that I expected to, but I rather fancied I'd bump into Julia or Simone at least, although so far I'd not seen a familiar face. Now whether that was a bad sign or not, I didn't know. Julia hadn't been in touch since I'd received her note and I'd had no reason to contact Simone. They were grown women, I was sure they could cope, and I shrugged the thought aside.

AnnaMaria was wrong about the drinks and the champagne was followed by good wine, which I denied myself as I wanted us to get home in one piece. The exotic non-alcoholic fruit punch was pretty good though.

We took our seats by the bar, having decided to finish our drinks before dinner and we sat back awhile to see how the other half lived. Unsurprisingly AnnaMaria was sneeringly indifferent to the opulence that surrounded her. Anne confided it was all a bit sickening to her and I had to agree.

'Like the MPs in the sleaze rows a while ago,' she whispered.

I leaned closer to Anne. 'Don't you think it's more like some of the novels you've lent me?'

A smile twitched at the corner of her mouth. 'Radclyffe?' she asked.

I grinned, we were on exactly the same wavelength. Taking her hand I kissed the back of it gently. ' "And that night they were not parted",' I quoted softly.

Anne threw back her lovely head and laughed and AnnaMaria, more literary than you would imagine, raised a smile.

We were still chuckling when the woman in the nine-teenth-century costume approached us. Quickly making assumptions that weren't necessarily so, she turned to me and said, 'Madam, your table is ready.'

'Looks like I'm butch tonight,' I said to my two fellow diners, and Anne got another fit of the giggles.

I extended my arm and Anne graciously took it,

fighting hysterics all the while. 'It's the champagne, honestly,' she confided, though I didn't believe her for a moment. The waitress, or whatever she was, led us to a table at the far reaches of the hall.

'They're frightened we'll show them up, being country bumpkins,' AnnaMaria snorted as we weaved our way across the room. The admiring glances that followed AnnaMaria's every move were noticed only by me. She was wonderfully oblivious to the stir she caused.

Our attendant helped us to our seats but any feelings of sophistication were quickly replaced by discomfort. Extravagance, after all, isn't something I'm particularly familiar with. Despite my Aunt Cynthia who, *in extremis*, had helped keep my chin firmly above water, for me struggle wasn't so far away that I'd forgotten what it was like.

And then I looked at Anne's face. The woman who had turned my life around was smiling at me, was delighted with me in fact, and the surreal surroundings suddenly didn't bother me at all.

'Do you know?' she said, eyes still full of humour, 'I keep expecting Marlene Dietrich to walk in.'

'There's one or two here about her age.' AnnaMaria's barbed comment had me choking on my juice and even Anne found it hard to suppress a smile.

'Don't be so ageist,' she scolded her niece.

'Well, look at the state of some of them.'

Beyond subtlety, we scanned the crowd as instructed. My earlier prediction of 'fat gits in tuxedos' proved to be inaccurate and while, as in most groups of women, all shapes, sizes and ages were represented, there did seem to be a predominance of older, sleeker and undoubtedly richer lesbians present. There was an international feel to the proceedings too; Simone's much-vaunted Japanese visitors being in evidence amongst the groups of women.

'Not exactly your average cross section of dykes is it?' AnnaMaria observed dryly.

'And what would that be?' I asked over my glass, dying to know what AnnaMaria's stereotypes would be. She gave me a haughty look and leaned across the table (we probably looked like the three witches in *Macbeth* at this point). 'Have you any idea how many lesbians are on my course?' she queried, her face breaking into a smile.

'*Touché*,' I laughed.

'I may be straight, but I'm not blind you know. Anyway never mind all that, I'm starving, let's eat.'

The meal was fabulous, if a little light. AnnaMaria looked as though she could have eaten three helpings. As our plates were whisked away, our glasses were refilled and despite her tendency to wind, AnnaMaria stuck to wine. Even she couldn't imagine drinking a pint in that company.

By ten o'clock I felt an urgency to be with Anne alone, away from a crowd of women with whom I had nothing in common. AnnaMaria had disappeared to the toilet and had been waylaid somewhere along the line, either that or there was a queue to end all queues.

Anne and I held hands across the table. 'I want to be at home with you,' she said, echoing my own thoughts. 'Any chance of sneaking off?'

'With or without your niece?' I smiled.

'With!' AnnaMaria bellowed behind me. 'Don't you dare leave me here.' She sat down with a sigh. Her cheeks were flushed and her shirt and tie were askew. 'I have just been talking to the most boring person in the universe,' she began and, flustered, ran her hand over her blonde crewcut.

'Anybody we know?' Anne asked, intrigued.

'I hope not, for your sake,' she replied. 'Bloody weird looking too, all arms, legs and smarmy smile.'

'Sounds gorgeous,' I commented. 'Just my type. What's she called?'

'Leisel.' She sneered as if that explained it all.

'Oh, yeah,' I said, recognising the name. 'Simone said she might come.'

'You know her?' AnnaMaria's lip curled in disgust.

My knowledge of the woman was obviously some sort of betrayal.

'No, no,' I said hastily. 'She owns one of the cars to be auctioned. Apparently she's overseeing the sale personally.'

'Perhaps she doesn't trust Simone,' Anne commented.

'Would you?' her niece replied, the curling lip still in evidence.

I tried not to think of the trust I'd already invested in Julia's two-timing, currently married, lover.

'Anyway,' I said, dismissing such doubts, 'what's she like, apart from rich?'

'And ugly,' Anne piped up.

'And ugly,' I corrected.

'See for yourself,' AnnaMaria said and an oily fingernail indicated Leisel's whereabouts.

Teutonic was my first thought. Blonde, blue-eyed and far from ugly, the reason for AnnaMaria's dislike wasn't immediately obvious. Simone and Julia were with her and together they made an intriguing threesome.

The new woman from South America and Simone, both tall cool blondes, were in startling contrast to Julia's dark, Mediterranean fire. Julia spotted us and waved.

'They're heading our way,' Anne murmured into my ear. Her breath drew goosebumps along my neck and I turned to face her. Her mouth was inches from mine and I couldn't resist kissing those full red lips. She kissed me back, any reserve having long since been drowned in wine.

'I'm off,' AnnaMaria interrupted our kiss. 'I'm not talking to that silly arse again.'

A steel hand clamped over her arm. 'Oh no, you're not,' Anne commanded.

To my utter amazement, AnnaMaria stayed uncomplainingly put. Beneath Anne's mild manner lay a will of iron. I couldn't wait to get to know her better!

'What did she say to you?' I quietly asked AnnaMaria.

'It's not so much what she said, it's what she did,' she replied mysteriously and stubbornly, looking away.

Bewildered, I looked at Anne, who, equally confused, raised an eyebrow in reply.

The three women, meanwhile, bore down on us. Julia's problems had been resolved, judging by the spring in her step, that and Simone's strategically placed grip on her arm. Leisel, she of the Germanic name and looks to match, sauntered closely behind.

Predictably, Julia wore an unadorned tuxedo and, equally predictably, Simone's dark blue ball gown, whilst bravely and spiritedly trying to restrain a pair of burgeoning breasts, outshone every other frock in the place. The flattering light emphasised the lushness of the velvet fabric and as she turned to speak to someone in the crowd, I could see her back was bare from neck to lower waist. God knows how she kept the dress on, gravity obviously isn't what it was.

The conversation with the stranger in the crowd lengthened and even from this distance I could see Simone was irritated. She waved her two companions on and took a chair at the table. Resentment oozed from every pore.

'Who's she talking to?' Anne asked, noticing the episode too.

'God knows,' I replied, 'but somebody's pissed her off.'

'Well, look what the cat dragged in,' AnnaMaria muttered.

'Come on then, sharpeyes,' I encouraged. 'Who's made her mad?'

AnnaMaria curled her lip, a gesture I'd become familiar with. 'Darling Caroline,' she said, with as much derision as she could muster. 'She's sat with some tight-arse in a frock.' Working in a garage had gone someway to adding to AnnaMaria's repertoire of insults.

It was barely perceptible, but Anne stiffened slightly. I felt an uncomfortable and sanity-threatening twinge of jealousy.

'The cow,' Anne whispered, which made me feel better. 'Who's she with?' she asked, which made me feel worse. I craned my neck; if she was with her other lover, I wanted an eyeful too.

I sat down with a thud. 'Good God, Jocelyn!'

'That's her, that's the woman I met,' Anne said thoughtfully.

'Yes, well I've met Jocelyn too, she's Simone's receptionist and from what I can tell they're welcome to each other.'

Anne suddenly laughed. 'I suppose I should thank her,' she said. 'This,' she continued, indicating our linked hands, 'may never have happened.'

'She knew you'd be here, you'd think she'd stay away,' AnnaMaria mumbled, glaring in Caroline's direction.

'It doesn't matter,' Anne said, and she squeezed my

fingers reassuringly. 'Anyway, how would she know I'd be here? I didn't tell her.'

'No,' her niece replied. 'I did.'

'What?' Anne said, patently surprised.

'I rang her and told her to, you know, keep away for a while.' AnnaMaria looked uncomfortable, recognising her gaffe.

'You warned her off, you mean.' Anne was close to anger, a side of her I'd never seen before, and her dark eyes flashed a warning.

AnnaMaria cleared her throat warily. 'Well, not in so many words . . .'

She was rescued from trying to explain her reasoning by the arrival of my former lover and her towering Teutonic friend.

AnnaMaria's body language was a psychologist's dream. From crossed legs and folded arms to rigid posture and terrifying scowl, her whole demeanour screamed 'Don't come near'.

Julia, so obviously brimming with news, missed these dynamics and made cheery introductions.

A manicured hand briefly gripped mine and shrewd blue eyes assessed my not-so-new suit and well-washed shirt. She lingered for a moment on Anne, who clearly met her approval. Anne's discomfort was plain. She'd told me that past experience had made her impervious to the shabby treatment meted out to her by men, but this was a whole new ball game. AnnaMaria needn't have worried about Leisel, the South Amercian's appraisal of her was quick and dismissive.

'Join us,' I offered, my upbringing preventing me from giving her a tempting slap in the chops.

'Thank you,' Leisel drawled and she draped herself elegantly into a chair. She sat to my right, immediately opposite Anne. Her eyes, more grey than blue I noted, flickered unashamedly across Anne's face and upper body. Anne folded her arms across her chest. Leisel smiled, and a dozen ice floes crashed together in the frozen Arctic tundra.

Julia was still oblivious to all that surrounded her. Or she didn't care. No doubt her business acumen enabled her to deal with all types. Whatever, she handled Leisel courteously enough. I suppose there was too much money riding on the auction not to.

The third member of the party was conspicuous by her absence, and from the corner of my eye I could see Simone still deep in conversation with Caroline. The hostess was taut and tense in her chair and as Leisel rambled on about this, her first trip to England, I half wished I was in a position to overhear the other conversation.

'. . . And of course I always fly business class, though on this occasion I was tempted to travel with the Mercedes. One hates to entrust one's valuables to others.'

I took another, closer look at Leisel. Despite the Swiss-taught, public-school accent, I thought perhaps she was joking, maybe practising her Frankie Howerd impersonation. But then I realised she was quite serious. What could I do but join in? I hadn't starred in my school plays for nothing.

'One can't be too careful,' I agreed in the best Windsor accent I could manage at such short notice. 'I have the same problems with my livestock.' Leisel looked intrigued, thinking, I was sure, that I was the owner of the next Grand National winner, though AnnaMaria's snort of laughter ruined the effect a bit.

Julia's stern look was a warning not to push it.

Further mischief was prevented by an unexpected announcement from the tannoy.

'Tonight's special guests, Ladies and Gentlemen . . .'

I glanced around. Could there be a man lurking in this sea of suits?

'She's being polite,' Julia murmured.

'Who to?' Anne hissed back.

'All the butch numbers in the audience.' AnnaMaria's comment signalled her desire to rejoin the party.

I stifled laughter as the MC droned on.

'. . . all the way from Scotland, the Edinburgh Ladies Dance Band.'

Applause greeted the announcement and the twenty-piece band of rather gorgeous Femmes Fatales took their place on stage and began to tune up.

Leisel, distracted by an attractive face in the crowd, excused herself and left the table. We breathed a collective sigh of relief. Even Julia seemed glad to be shot of her. AnnaMaria simply tutted at her departing back.

'Thank God she's gone. She's been driving me mad all day. Even Simone's sick of her,' Julia complained.

'So you're back on then?' I asked and signalled to the waitress for more drinks. Julia's stories were too good to hear on an empty glass.

'Of course,' Julia smiled.

'What about the husband?' Anne asked, intrigued despite an aversion to gossip (unlike me, who liked nothing better).

'Richard, you mean?' Julia replied, looking smug.

AnnaMaria, with a replenished plate courtesy of the waitress, was suddenly distracted from her favourite occupation of feeding her face.

'Richard Steigel?' she asked, through a crusty bread roll.

Julia nodded, and was either amazed that AnnaMaria might possibly know her lover's husband or that someone could still speak with that amount of food inside their mouth.

'Do you know him?' Anne asked.

'No,' she replied and drank some wine.

'Oh,' I murmured, vaguely disappointed by her response.

'I don't,' she continued, 'but Andy does. He's in his motorbike club. Camp as Christmas, apparently.' Subject closed, she wrestled with another tasty morsel from her plate.

Julia beamed. 'Yep, he's as queer as a coot. A marriage of convenience, Simone says. It kept their respective families happy, they're a bit conservative in that part of Sweden.'

'But I thought you said they were sleeping together.' Events had taken an unexpected turn for me.

'Well, trust me, they're not. He's more likely to sleep with Andy than Simone.'

AnnaMaria paused to see how she was expected to take that comment but shrugged it off, perhaps she didn't care if he did.

'Is that it then?' I asked, exasperated.

Julia brushed an errant curl of hair out of her eye before answering. 'Well, what's to tell? I asked her what the score was and she told me.'

I could have hit her. 'Do they live together, work together, how long have they been married? Oh come on, Julia!' She'd been in such a state I couldn't just let her shrug it off. But shrug it off she did.

'I've told you, it's fine. He's gay, he seems a nice enough bloke. I've only met him the once . . .'

'I'll ask Andy,' AnnaMaria piped up, obviously as tired of this bullshit story as I was.

'You could always ask me.' Simone's sudden presence and clipped accent startled us all.

Her life uncluttered by tact, AnnaMaria said 'Okay, so I'm asking.'

Unfazed, and I suspect a little impressed, Simone laughed. She held out her be-ringed hand. 'And you are?'

'AnnaMaria.'

'Ah yes,' Simone said grasping the oily outstretched hand. 'Anne's niece.' She paused briefly. 'Anne, Letty, I'm so pleased you could come. Sorry I wasn't here to meet you, but I had business to attend to.'

The clichés rolled off her tongue thick and fast.

'Yes, I noticed Caroline was here.' Anne's comment surprised me as anger peppered her words. Simone smoothly broke the awkward silence.

'Her business is with my husband rather than me. I'm sorry if you find her presence . . . difficult.' Another calculated pause. 'I know you were close.'

'Nothing I can't cope with,' Anne replied frostily.

'What is his business?' AnnaMaria asked pointedly.

The conversation wasn't quite following the polite circles of chit chat I had been expecting. I still didn't know how Leisel had wound AnnaMaria up, but Simone was getting it in the neck on her behalf.

But Simone was older and wiser and a slip of a girl would not be allowed to get the better of her. She took the chair vacated by Leisel and shifted her charm machine into second gear.

'He's my associate,' Simone began, carefully giving AnnaMaria her full attention.

'So you're the boss then?' AnnaMaria pressed. I was beginning to think I'd actually learn something here.

Simone smiled, well her lips turned up but her eyes were cautious, rather guarded. 'No, not exactly, it's more of a partnership. Our firm has expanded, we have international interests now and an international reputation to go with it.' Her smile was suddenly more genuine. Her work was important to her and the pleasure it gave her was evident on her face. 'He works mostly in Europe, my contacts are in the States and South America. It works well for us . . .'

'And you only have to be a dyke when you want to be,' AnnaMaria said dryly. 'It's a great set up. Keeps everybody happy, except maybe your lover.'

'AnnaMaria!' Anne butted in, shocked out of silence.

Her niece conceded a point. 'I'm sorry,' she said, pushing her plate away. 'But I can't understand all these guessing games. If you want to know something it always seems easiest just to ask.'

'Fair enough,' Anne agreed. 'But the comments about Simone's private life were a bit below the belt.'

AnnaMaria stubbornly shook her head. 'But it's more than that, don't you see?' She looked Simone straight in the eye. 'It's game playing, fitting in when it suits. Straight with family and most of your business contacts, gay with your lover and when you feel safe, like tonight. This is the nineties remember, you don't have to put up with that bullshit anymore, especially a woman in your position.'

Our party fell silent at AnnaMaria's outburst. Simone looked as though someone had slapped her and even Julia was momentarily lost for words. Face flushed, Simone got to her feet. Composure coldly back in place, she said, 'If you'll excuse me, I must mingle.'

We watched her walk away. She'd already had words with Caroline, had been stressed out with Leisel and now, with an onslaught from an opinionated seventeen-year-old, it really hadn't been Simone's day.

Julia suddenly laughed. 'Are you sure you want to be a mechanic? Wouldn't a job in politics be better?'

'God, no,' AnnaMaria retorted. 'They can't handle the truth at all. She may not have liked it, but at least Simone listened.'

'I'll go and soothe some ruffled feathers I think,' Julia said. 'I'd better keep an eye on Leisel too. God, knows what she'll be up to.' Julia grabbed her glass and took off after her lover.

'I've got an idea what Leisel will be doing,' Anna-Maria sniffed.

'Okay then,' I said, smiling, remembering her earlier words, 'I'm asking.'

'Well,' she replied, 'I'm pretty certain that when I saw her in the bog it wasn't snuff she was stuffing up her nose.'

Chapter 12

'My God!' Anne said over the music. 'Drugs. Cocaine! Do you think AnnaMaria was right?'

I twirled Anne around the dance floor and carefully concentrated on not crushing her feet. She was a much better dancer than me and she deftly avoided my clumsy manoeuvres.

'Probably,' I said absently. 'You know what these rich types are like.'

'Well she certainly lives in the right part of the world if it's cocaine she's into.'

I laughed as the music soared. Abruptly Anne changed the subject. 'You know,' she said, 'we've never done this before.'

'What?' I asked, changing direction to avoid a tailored buxom pair bearing down on us.

'Danced,' Anne explained.

I held her tighter and smiled at her pretty open features. 'I've never danced with someone quite so delectable.'

'You flatterer you,' she said and leaned closer to kiss me. My rhythm was lost altogether then and we juddered to a halt. The buxom couple slammed into us.

Apologies were made and Anne reluctantly led me from the dance floor.

'It's true though,' I said as we returned to our table. 'You are utterly gorgeous.'

'In the two years I've known you I never suspected you possessed such charm,' Anne teased, holding my hand. She only released it when the music stopped and she clapped as the mixed bunch of dancers drifted back to their seats.

'You've got lots to learn about me yet,' I replied. 'My inability to dance is just one of them.'

My heart tripped over itself as she whispered, 'Well there's no rush is there?' and smiled.

Thus engrossed I never noticed AnnaMaria return to the table. In truth I'd not seen her leave either. She cleared her throat to get my attention.

'I hope you haven't been mixing with drug-crazed lesbians again,' I scolded mockingly, before she had a chance to speak.

'The crazy and the lesbian I can cope with,' she said. 'It's the drugs that do my head in.'

'I didn't know you had such strong feelings about it,' I said, mistakenly presuming that everyone under thirty treated Ecstasy, Acid and dope as a kind of fashion statement. Anne's niece was proving me quite wrong. Perhaps I shouldn't judge everyone by my own standards.

'You know my sister was killed in a car crash,' Anne said. 'Well, the driver was on drugs.'

'Ah,' I said, understanding a little more and suddenly glad my days of recreational drug use were over. I'm not being pompous, my efforts at grow your own in Yorkshire were such a disaster I'd given it up as a bad job.

'You can see why it pisses me off,' AnnaMaria explained.

'Where did you get to anyway?' Anne asked. The change of tack was effortless, with no underlying awkwardness. It was obviously a conversation they were used to having and, though the dead woman's memory lived on, it was apparent that the pain of loss had receded with time.

'I've been in the kitchens,' AnnaMaria explained her disappearance.

'Not more food?' I exclaimed, wondering where she put it all.

She laughed and her sometimes rather serious face lit up. Suddenly I could see more clearly the family resemblance with Anne.

'No,' she chuckled. 'I've organised a carry out for Andy.'

The thought of Simone subsidising Andy's dinner somehow seemed hilarious, though I wasn't quite sure why. The joke appealed to my companions too and soon we were all three giggling into our drinks.

Julia rejoined us an hour later and she conducted a private, almost intimate conversation with AnnaMaria. I didn't take much notice, I was having intimacies of my own with Anne.

Suddenly the MC announced a further special guest. Well actually, she announced two.

'From Canada,' the announcement began, 'last year's World Latin American Dance champions, Mark and Marcia Trudeaux!'

'I thought this was women only,' I said as Mark and Marcia took to the dance floor.

'It is, you silly sod,' Julia bellowed over the applause. 'Where the hell have you been the last two years?'

I craned for a better look and I could just about make

out 'Mark's' breasts. A strange addition to the goatee beard. 'Christ,' I said quietly as the couple began their routine.

Though not an aficionado of 'Come Dancing', even I could see they were experts in their field. Every toe in the place was tapping and the enthusiastic band gave fire to their performance.

They slipped neatly into the rhumba and we were spellbound. The music reached its crescendo and with customary false smiles stuck to their faces and chests heaving with their efforts they left the floor to a standing ovation.

'Right, Ladies,' the band leader piped up in her warm Scottish drawl. 'Have we any couples for the tango?'

'I can do that,' AnnaMaria muttered. 'Come on,' she said, turning to Julia, 'you've been bragging about your dancing skills all night. Let's see what you can do.' Not one to be denied she grabbed Julia by the hand and hauled her under the spotlights.

This I had to see.

Images of *Sunset Boulevard* accompanied their solo spot. A red rose between clenched teeth was all that was missing. Julia, for all her boasting, was outdanced in every way and the audience, egged on, I imagined, by lustful thoughts, gave them a cheer that rivalled the Canadian couple's departure.

AnnaMaria glowed and Julia looked completely knackered when they were finally allowed to leave the floor.

'My God!' I turned to AnnaMaria. 'That was amazing. Where did you learn to do that?'

In reply she bowed to her aunt and Anne smiled at the theatrics.

'You? Really?' I said, though I don't know why I was

so surprised. Anne's dancing had shown more than a little flair.

'Me and my sister used to go to dance lessons when we were children. My mother insisted and we both showed some talent for it. I've been teaching Anna-Maria for about a year now. She's got the same grace her mother had.'

'Yeah,' AnnaMaria enthused. 'Mum won loads of awards too. I've still got all her cups and medals.'

'Don't you fancy taking it up, maybe doing it professionally?' Julia asked, duly impressed.

'Hell no, I'd have to wear those fucking horrible frocks. I prefer a smart tuxedo myself.'

It was a mystery to me why AnnaMaria wasn't a dyke. It was exactly what I and a thousand other lesbians would have said.

'Do you mind if we go soon?' AnnaMaria asked checking her watch. 'It's nearly one and I've got college tomorrow.'

'It's okay with me,' I said and turned to Anne who nodded her agreement. 'Seeing as you haven't got work tomorrow,' I continued quietly, 'how do you fancy staying at mine tonight?' Lust flittered across her face, I took that as a 'yes'.

'Go, go,' Julia said wearily. 'And take the Dancing Queen with you.'

'Thank Simone for me, would you?' Anne asked, rising to her feet. 'And if I don't see you before, I'll see you at the auction.'

'Oh, you'll be going then?' Julia asked.

'Wouldn't miss it for the world.'

We retrieved our coats as AnnaMaria skipped off to fetch Andy's lunchbox. On our way out we had the misfortune of bumping into a stressed Caroline heading alone into the night. Nothing was said as she raced past us and the darkened streets of Manchester swallowed her hurrying form.

Chapter 13

I deposited AnnaMaria on her doorstep and took Anne home with me.

'It didn't bother me you know, seeing Caroline,' Anne explained on the winding journey home.

I smiled with relief as I negotiated the narrow lanes. 'I'm glad,' I said. 'I didn't want it to be a problem for us.'

Anne snorted derisively. 'No way,' she said. 'I was just worried you might think I was using you to, oh I don't know, to make me feel better or needed again or something . . .' she finished lamely.

I glanced at her in the darkened car. The occasional street light was reflected in her eyes and she was clearly troubled. 'Anne, I never thought that for a moment. I'm just glad it's me you want to be with.'

'Trust me, Letty. As far as Caroline is concerned she's welcome to her new woman. I've gone from sad to mad and as for us, well, I've admired you for years. Fancied you too, on and off. Was there any wonder I'd die of embarrassment every time I saw you?' She smiled wryly.

I laughed. 'Same here, except it took me a bit longer to figure it out.'

Anne's arm crept around the back of my neck and her cool hand fondling my warm skin did strange things to everything below my waist.

Her lurid suggestions whispered directly into my ear did nothing for my driving skills either. Whatever had happened to the shy woman I used to know?

'Where did you learn to talk like that?' I teased her.

'I've told you before I'm not as innocent as Anna-Maria would have you believe. I don't work in a library for nothing, you know? Lesbian writing didn't start and end with Radclyffe Hall. I've read all the books you have, and more.' She smiled as memory overtook her.

Minutes later we arrived home and as we hopped out of the vehicle all was silent except for the Land Rover's cooling engine and the gentle 'cluck-cluck' from Henrietta, who, strangely, was asleep atop the outhouse roof and not on her coop as usual.

The rain had eased as the evening had worn on but the damp October night was heavy and oppressive. Thunder rumbled ominously in the distance, another downpour was imminent.

I dug in my coat pocket for my house keys. 'Shit,' I mumbled as they eluded my grasp and then I realised they were beyond my reach simply because they weren't there.

'Letty,' Anne said quietly. 'The door's open.'

An icy bolt of fear had me immobilised for a few seconds. Memories of Manchester's mean streets were never far away and my first instinct to run was hard to ignore. Finally I forced my reluctant feet into action, but Anne, my hero, beat me to it. She gestured for me to be silent as she tiptoed through the unlocked door and into the kitchen.

The standard lamp that always burned at night threw off its customary glow and though everything looked normal enough, instinctively I knew that someone had been in my house.

We searched the rooms together and fear rather than Anne's presence accelerated my heart beat. There was nothing to see, nothing seemed to be missing. My credit cards and cash were on my dresser where I'd left them. It was odd, I felt as though someone had come in for a look around and then left.

Several things clinched that idea. A familiar smell had dogged me during the search. Anne whispered she could smell something too, though she couldn't put her finger on it. The stub of a Gauloise by the side of my bed confirmed my suspicions. Julia's brand, but not her cigarette, unless she'd arrived by helicopter, which seemed unlikely, though on reflection she still had spare keys to my house.

We shuffled downstairs after examining the upstairs rooms. Anne put the kettle on as I searched my coat pocket. Of course my keys were hidden in the lining. I threw the yard lights on to illuminate outdoors and Erik awoke with a squawk. Anne dropped a mug in shock. She chuckled nervously. 'I feel like Sherlock Holmes,' she said. 'Are you sure you didn't have a cig before you came out?' This had been Anne's line of thinking as we'd wandered nervously through the house.

'No, I only smoke under extreme conditions. I could do with one now,' I added quietly. I settled for a brandy instead and took one to Anne, who, strangely, was up to the elbows in suds at the sink.

'You smoke, I wash,' she answered my unspoken question.

'Have a drink instead,' I said. 'I can't afford to lose any more crockery.'

To my relief she laughed and, drying her hands on a tea towel, took a seat across the big pine table. The brandy hit me like a sledgehammer and I immediately felt better.

'Are you going to ring the police?' Anne asked.

'I dunno, what do you think?' My decision-making abilities had floated away.

'Probably,' she said. 'Maybe there's some dangerous French lunatic on the loose.'

I was glad she could joke, though the idea of a lunatic, of any nationality, on my premises was rather worrying.

I took her advice and rang the local station. Sam, the bobby who controlled these parts, was on night duty. I was glad I could talk to someone I knew. He had no knowledge of escaped burglars who didn't steal anything, French or otherwise, and he tried to convince me I'd left the door open when I went out. I was half inclined to believe him, though the remains of the cigarette was still a mystery.

He offered to call but I decided morning would do. I took his advice to lock up tight but drew the line at getting a guard dog. Fairly impractical at three o'clock in the morning anyway.

Anne had poured another generous amount of brandy when I got back to the kitchen. I briefed her on the conversation.

'Are you okay?' she asked.

I waved my glass at her. 'Getting better by the minute.'

'Let's go to bed,' she suggested and thoughts of unwelcome house guests flew out of the window. Later my body shook with pleasure rather than nerves as we explored our growing repertoire of lovemaking.

Checking the bread knife was to hand, I had a peaceful, post-orgasmic sleep.

We awoke three hours later to Erik's screeches. His

sleep had been less than perfect, the yard lights had obviously kept him awake all night and Henrietta hadn't been there to soothe him. Banishing thoughts of intruders, I switched to automatic pilot, saw to the hens, stuck the kettle on the Aga and absently emptied the sink of cold, sudsy water. Staring blearily out of the kitchen window I spotted something I'd missed the night before. Tyre tracks ran along the length of the gravel drive. The marks were new, I'd only raked the path the evening before.

Whoever had visited had driven as far as the chicken run, reversed and driven out again. The tracks crossed each other further down the path. I pulled my dressing gown tighter around my shoulders and went out for a closer look. The promised rain had begun to fall and I grabbed my golfers' brolly on the way.

I must have looked a sight, bent over tyre tracks that were rapidly being washed away by the pounding rain. Whatever, I looked bad enough to nearly give Sam the Policeman a seizure. Him and me both.

'For God's sake, Sam, you frightened me to death, sneaking up on me like that.'

'Sorry,' he said. 'I could say the same thing though. What are you doing out here, Letty? I thought you'd have been barricaded in by now.'

Sam, middle-aged and miserable by nature, stomped into the kitchen. Water cascaded from his rain cape all over the kitchen floor. Tutting, I rescued the screaming kettle from the hot ring.

'Tea?' I demanded.

'Coffee?' he asked hopefully.

I slammed about in an effort to get myself under control.

'What were you doing exactly?' he asked, reaching for a steaming mug.

'Looking at tyre tracks,' I muttered, mopping the rain-streaked floor irritably.

'Any particular reason?' Sam pressed, lifting his feet as I mopped around him.

'We had intruders last night, in case you'd forgotten.'

'We?' he asked curiously.

'Don't be nosey,' I said, slinging the mop and bucket back in the cupboard.

Sam eased back in his chair, both hands wrapped around his mug. It looked as though he was here for the duration.

'Aren't you going to take notes?' I asked, leaning against the Aga for warmth.

'If you want,' he said amiably enough.

'Look Sam, you're not taking this very seriously.'

'Oh, but I am,' he replied, grey moustache hiding a mouth itching to smile. He finally put his mug down and produced a pad and pen. 'Right,' he began. 'So what time did you get home?'

He took brief notes as I retold the previous night's experiences. It was impossible not to mention Anne and only one raised furry eyebrow expressed any sort of interest. The more I dwelt on events, the more idiotic it sounded. Someone had been in my house, of that I was sure, but the fact that nothing had been disturbed or stolen made the occurrence seem strange, a little odd, rather than life threatening.

Sam closed his notepad with a decisive snap. 'I'll look into it, Letty and if I hear of any similar incidents I'll be in touch. I wouldn't hold your breath though,' he added as an afterthought.

It was all I'd been expecting and I escorted him back to his bike parked near the front door. I couldn't resist a glance at the drive as we walked past. Only a ghost of

117

the tyre tracks remained, the rain had quite thoroughly washed away any evidence.

'No car?' I asked as he swung his leg over the crossbar.

'I was on my way home,' he said. 'Just thought I'd drop in. Save WPC Auckland a trip later.'

That was a shame. Emma Auckland, a dyke if ever I saw one, was new to the area and I'd been itching to meet her. I gave Sam a wave as he trundled off on his bike and distracted, I let myself back into the house.

Anne was up and about. Bright-eyed and bushy-tailed, despite too much wine, sex and a nasty fright the night before. She wore a lovely soft grey woollen jumper and her jeans were the Pepe's she'd bought on our shopping trip, now fading to a nice worn blue.

'So you came prepared did you?' I asked, slipping into her arms. The wool tickled my nose but she was so warm and soft, sexy to the touch, that an itchy nose wasn't going to stop me. We cuddled for a while and she kissed me, gently arousing all the feelings that were gradually growing within me. She smelt gorgeous, of clean hair and teeth and a touch of my Eau Savage behind her ears.

'Let me go for a shower,' I pleaded, pulling away. 'I feel disgustingly filthy by the side of you.'

'You smell of bed,' she said, refusing to let go. She sniffed loudly. 'And chickens!'

'Exactly,' I laughed. 'Come and talk to me while I shower. I'll tell you what Sam the Man had to say.'

Needless to say Anne joined me in the shower and it was fully an hour before we returned to the kitchen.

A lorry of gigantic proportions blotted out the day-light from the kitchen window and someone was frantically banging on the back door.

Chapter 14

'Where do you want this lot then?' the man demanded.

Small and rotund, the driver of the lorry peered at me through glasses, the lenses of which were so scratched it was a wonder he could see me, never mind the road.

'What lot?' I asked glancing at the unmarked vehicle.

He sighed, it was eight a.m. and he'd obviously dealt with fools at this time of the morning before.

'The marquee,' he explained slowly.

My blank look must have tried his patience.

'Here,' he said and shoved an oily, crumpled delivery note into my hand. It read, 'Marquee, Type 4, Ms L. Campbell, Calderton Brook Farm. Floored Auction spec.'

Gobbledegook, but auction rang a bell of course. 'Come in,' I instructed the driver. 'I've just got to make a call.'

He stomped into the kitchen, his two burly mates in tow, and they took a seat at the table as a somewhat bemused Anne made tea.

'I'll just ring Julia,' I whispered to her. 'See what's going on.'

I nipped into the hall and rang her mobile phone

number. I'm sure she slept with the thing under her pillow and chances were she'd answer it.

A sleepy voice answered after the fifth ring. 'Yep?' she asked.

'Julia, it's Letty.'

'Hiya,' she mumbled, still not with it.

I didn't beat about the bush. 'I've got three blokes here with a marquee . . .'

'Shit, shit, shit.' Suddenly she was wide awake. 'It's for the auction.'

'I gathered as much, what exactly am I supposed to do with it?'

'Sorry, Letty,' she replied. 'I was supposed to explain last night, but I forgot all about it.'

I could hear clattering noises in the background as Julia raced from room to room. I could picture her posh flat in Salford Quays and I was with her every step of the way as she filled the kettle.

'Look, I'll be over in about an hour and a half. Take them to the bottom fields. They've got plans, they should know what they're doing. They can make a start.'

'Julia!' I began, annoyed with her.

'Letty, I'll be there as soon as I can. Bye.'

The phone went dead.

She was right about my visitors having plans. They were discussed at great length over several cups of tea. My stash of tea bags was diminishing by the second. We were already onto dried milk.

Charlie, who was both the foreman and the driver, seeing that no more refreshments were forthcoming, folded the plans decisively and ushered his staff back to the lorry.

'We'll do the shell first,' he attempted to explain,

'now the rain's stopped. And tomorrow we'll be back to make a start on the flooring. Is that okay?'

I shrugged. I'd had no involvement in any of it. I was amazed I was being consulted at all. The hens were reluctant to go back into their enclosure, but I couldn't leave them out; they were stupid enough to head straight for the lorry's wheels.

An odd thought occurred and I called to Charlie before he could leave. 'You weren't here last night by any chance, were you?'

'Not us, love,' he assured me gruffly. 'Our instructions were for delivery this morning.' And with that he drove off.

A glance at the lorry's tyres did nothing to confirm or deny his comment. Any comparative wheel imprints had long since disappeared. With a sigh I realised it was a mystery I was never likely to solve.

I checked for eggs as Charlie drove off and I was surprised to draw a blank. Whatever had happened last night had disturbed them enough not to lay and Henrietta, still reluctant to join her pals, surveyed all from the outhouse roof.

I watched Charlie manoeuvre his lorry down the road toward the fields. My Aunt Cynthia, in her wisdom, had ensured the road was wide enough for farm vehicles, though as far as I was aware nothing bigger than my Land Rover and its detachable trailer had ever been down it.

Julia arrived half an hour later, just as I was kissing Anne goodbye on the doorstep. The last twenty-four hours had been exhausting and she confessed she was knackered and wanted to go home for a kip.

'I didn't know going out with you would be such a whirlwind,' she said, laughing. 'You'd think being a

121

chicken farmer in Yorkshire would be a peaceful, quiet sort of occupation.'

'It used to be, believe me,' I said. 'Anyway, when can I see you again?'

'Friday?' she suggested.

I smiled. 'Fine, come here for tea if you want. We can view the marquee by the setting sun.'

She strode off, laughing and waved cheerily to Julia who was busy gabbing on her mobile phone. Julia waved back absently.

For a woman who, only an hour or two before, had been cosily tucked up in bed thirty miles way, Julia looked remarkably well turned out. And for a change she'd even dressed for the occasion. A fern green roll-neck cashmere sweater ensured the chilly morning air would be kept at bay and a contrasting green waxed jacket would repel any amount of rain. Cream jodhpurs and brown leather riding boots completed the ensemble. Princess Anne, eat your heart out.

'They've gone down to the fields,' I called from the doorway.

'Right, I'll go and see how they're getting on,' she shouted back and turned to climb into her car.

'Hang on,' I waved to her and scuttled across the damp driveway.

She paused in mid-step and waited for me to join her. 'Look, I'm sorry I didn't explain . . .' she began.

I reassured her. 'No, it's okay,' and leaned against the car's gleaming paintwork as I gathered my thoughts. 'New?' I asked, admiring the BMW.

'Not to me,' she said wistfully. 'I had to borrow Simone's, mine's in for a service. Anyway, what's up?'

I explained about my intruders of the previous night. She laughed when I mentioned the Gauloise.

'I didn't come down for a midnight drive, if that's

'what you're thinking,' she said, unperturbed by my insinuations.

'No, it's not that. I was just wondering if you've still got my spare house key?' I was clutching at straws by this time.

'Of course,' Julia replied, dangling the car keys in front of me.

'They're Simone's,' I pointed out.

'Oh God, yes. Sorry, but don't worry, they're still with my others. I doubt if my mechanic would decide to drive here either. Was anything stolen?'

'No, nothing was touched as far as I can see. Sam said he'd look into it.'

Julia smiled, she knew the policeman of old. 'Look, come down to the fields with me. Let's see how they're getting on with the marquee, we can talk on the way.'

I retrieved my coat from the house and seconds later eased my way into the leather luxury of Simone's car.

'Are you sure it was cocaine?' Julia asked as we drove through the farm.

She'd been surprised when I'd told her of Leisel's habit. 'AnnaMaria seemed to think so, though she didn't look stoned.'

'Perhaps you don't on cocaine,' Julia commented. 'Sod her, anyway. After showing her the sights and wining and dining her all day yesterday, I don't care if she burns her brain and rots her nostrils. As long as it's after the auction,' she added.

'That good, eh?' I prodded.

'Worse, far worse. My God, I don't know how I didn't throttle her. Even Simone lost her patience in the end. Self-centred, self-satisfied, stuck-up cow.'

'AnnaMaria wasn't very impressed either,' I said, gazing out of the window. 'Is she a dyke then?' I asked, recalling Leisel's interest in Anne.

'Bisexual, according to Simone. Wouldn't touch her with a bargepole myself. Caroline was all over her, though.'

'Really?' I asked, surprised by this piece of information. 'I thought she was seeing Jocelyn.'

'She is, but she's an opportunist. The three of them are very pally. They didn't leave together, though.'

'I know,' I said. 'Caroline left when we did. How did that all happen?'

'Dunno,' Julia said. 'You know what the gay scene is like. Bedhopping is something we seem to excel at.'

'You speak for yourself,' I laughed.

Julia sighed. 'Leisel's off to Russia after the auction. I can't imagine Caroline globetrotting after her.'

'I wish she would. She does seems a threat somehow.' I confessed a hidden fear.

'Give over,' Julia spluttered. 'Anne adores you, it's obvious. You never could see what's in front of your face. Hey look,' she said, pointing through the windscreen, 'the marquee's up.'

And indeed it was. An enormous structure imposing itself on the countryside. It was far bigger than I'd imagined. Of gaudy reds and yellows, it looked for all the world as though the circus had come to town.

Julia parked the car and we trudged across the hard-packed earth. The drainage was particularly good at this end of the farm and I could hear excess water from the fierce downpour gurgling happily into the stream that skirted the southern end of the land.

We surveyed the marquee from a slight incline and the merry structure billowed in the breeze. Sounds of hammering accompanied the flapping of canvas not yet tethered down and I felt a brief twinge of excitement. It all reminded me so much of fairs I'd been to as a

124

child. The memory quite took my breath away and I suddenly wished I was four again.

Julia went into the marquee to perform a little professional bullying and left me to reminisce.

Chapter 15

As the week went by Julia's visits became more frequent, and the sounds of activity grew louder and more insistent. So much wood was carted across the farm I was beginning to think Noah had paid a call.

Anne arrived on the Friday as promised and, caught a bit short in the shopping department, we had to settle for omelettes. My cholesterol level had to be at an all-time high, but we had to eat something.

The hens had thoughtfully started laying again and I even had enough to warrant a trip to the corner shop in Calderton. The gossip would be at screaming pitch by now, what with all the toing and froing. It was time I added fuel to the fire.

Foregoing the pleasures of a moonlit marquee we had a few beers and watched a video instead; Lily Savage in Concert had us howling with laughter. All in all, a typical lezzy night in.

Our lovemaking was less frantic that night somehow. I dismissed any worries over Caroline and relaxed into this new relationship. We chatted into the early hours and Anne fell asleep first, curled up at the side of me, head on my shoulder. I stroked her thick dark hair for a while until sleep crept in and took me to another land.

We did manage to get a look at the marquee the following day, and its progress was remarkable. Fully erected at thirty feet high it could be seen from miles around. Inside, a full floor of wood would keep the potential punters' feet well away from mother earth.

Surrounding the main event dozens of wooden platforms had been built, no doubt to house the cars that were due to arrive the following week. The long-range weather forecast had been promising. There seemed to be no reason why the auction shouldn't be a rip-roaring success.

Erik had followed us from the farm and pottered behind us as we examined the various structures. Perhaps he'd been Lassie in a previous life. He busily kicked up soil in his unrelenting search for grubs and other tasty morsels. It was revolting to watch.

Hand in hand we wandered around the field (me and Anne, not me and Erik). Anne asked if she could stay the weekend. I was so delighted I could hardly speak, so I kissed her 'yes' instead.

'Let's go to Calderton,' she suggested, leading me back to the house. 'I don't think I can stand a diet of eggs all weekend.'

'Are you criticising my culinary skills?' I mocked.

'Well, they don't call you Fanny for nothing.'

'You cheeky bitch,' I shrieked as she ran off laughing.

'Here, catch,' I called.

Curiosity caused her to turn in mid-stride and one of the eggs I'd collected earlier caught her neatly at the side of her head.

For a moment I thought I'd overdone it, her look of shock was one to behold. But I'd not misjudged her and a sod of earth flew back in response; my clean blue jeans were promptly filthy. I raced after her to the house, eggs and earth flying. The hours that followed were surely heaven sent.

Calderton was alive with rumour. How the natives had missed the signs of an impending auction was beyond me. Apart from leafleting every house, I was at a loss to know how the message could have been clearer.

Mrs Buckham, she of the corner shop, radiated curiosity. The amazing price she offered for my few trays of eggs was tantamount to bribery. In a gesture unknown to the residents of this small village, she doled out free tea and buns to me and Anne. But information isn't so cheap and I held out for a top up and a further toasted teacake.

She had an unprecedented amount of customers that particular Saturday afternoon as well, no doubt attracted by my Land Rover parked outside.

'And how's work coming along on your place?' Mrs Buckham asked, as she bustled about serving customers, many of whom she hadn't seen for years.

'Fine, fine,' I said, swirling the dregs of tea in my cup.

She rushed around the counter to fill it from an old earthenware pot she kept for special guests. And special I felt indeed. In these parts it was customary to treat newcomers like a virulent disease, at arm's length and with a grimace. My Aunt Cynthia may have made her home here, but a hundred and fifty years had to elapse before you were classed as local.

Curiosity had a strange way of overcoming such boundaries. Mrs Buckham, succumbing to pressure, I was sure, from members of the WI, was honour bound to ask.

'Is it ostriches?' was the unexpected opening gambit.

Anne somehow managed to remain expressionless.

'Sorry?' I said.

Lowering her voice to a whisper, Mrs Buckham added, 'Well, I know they're a delicacy in some parts. I prefer a nice piece of beef myself. I don't believe all those rumours, you know.'

'Oh?' Anne offered encouragement.

Mrs Buckham lowered her voice even more, lest her neighbours get an earful. 'Mad cow disease,' she explained. 'I've been eating it all my life and I'm as sane as the next person.'

I glanced around the shop. To be honest it wasn't saying much.

'They probably take a lot of looking after?' she questioned.

'I suppose,' I said through a mouthful of teacake. 'Milking must be a problem.'

Mrs Buckham looked puzzled. 'Oh, I didn't know you had to milk them, I thought they were like giant chickens.'

The woman was madder than I'd first thought.

Anne looked thoughtfully through the window. Her tiny Adam's apple bobbed up and down. Hysterics was near, I could tell.

Mrs Buckham pulled up a bar stool, liberated when the Dog and Partridge had burnt down some years ago, and sat down beside us. Her crimplene dress rode up around her thighs, revealing an expanse of firm and pale flesh.

'Don't they lay eggs?' she enquired.

'Cows?' I asked, thinking maybe I'd picked up the disease myself.

'No,' she explained slowly. 'You know, ostriches.'

'Yes, I think so. I don't really know much about them.'

Mrs Buckham was stumped for a moment. 'I suppose you can learn most things from books nowadays,' she concluded. 'You'd be able to help in that department, Miss Marple,' she said brightly, motioning to a bewildered Anne. She grabbed the teapot and headed for her small kitchen through the curtains that separated her home from the shop.

Beyond self-control, Anne let out a yelp of laughter. I feigned uninterest as every eye in the shop turned our way.

'Do you have anything on ostriches at the library?' I asked, politely.

Anne spluttered again. Her face had gone an alarming shade of red. I whacked her on the back and explained to the silent onlookers, 'Teacake. Down the wrong hole,' and smiled.

As a body, the customers resumed their quiet muttering and just the odd comment floated my way.

'Yorkshire weather 'ed kill 'em off,' one gruff voice commented.

'Aren't they from Peru, or is that guinea pigs?' said another.

'Come on,' Anne said, eyes wet with tearful laughter. 'I can't stand it anymore,' and she dragged me out of the shop.

Tempted as I was to prolong the agony, I relented and stuck a couple of flyers up in the shop window. Before we'd even driven ten yards the locals were around the window like buzzards, or even curious ostriches.

We decided to pay a quick call to the police station. Though I'd not mentioned the auction to Sam during his recent visit, one way or another word would have got to him by now and it seemed wise to advise him of my plans.

The station, a nineteenth-century converted terraced house sandwiched between the local butchers and a baker's of some renown, was a three-man show, or to be more specific, a one-woman-and-two-men show. Sergeant Sam headed a team of two other officers. WPC Auckland and PC Jerry Gordon. Emma the dyke was at the counter and her brief look of recognition was enough to confirm my suspicions. She was welcoming enough, if a little gruff, and she carefully took notes as I explained my visit.

Her fair hair was cut fashionably long in a bob that ended at her jaw. She tucked it neatly behind one small ear as she leaned over her notepad and scribbled away. 'We were notified of the auction just this morning,' she said.

'We were worried traffic might be a problem. Quite a few visitors are expected.'

'It's okay,' the policewoman said. 'Sergeant Mason's got it in hand.' She pronounced the word 'Sar'nt', the silent 'g' prompting the idea that she'd been in the forces at some point. If there is an army type, Emma was it. Tall, five foot ten maybe, muscular under the blue serge and ramrod straight. Dykes of my persuasion, if not me, would snap her up.

'The sergeant,' that silent 'g' again, 'won't be in till five. I'll let him know you called.'

Thus dismissed we headed for the door. But before I could leave she called out, 'Any more problems at the farm? I heard you had a break in.'

'No,' I replied. 'All quiet on the South-West front.'

She granted us a benevolent smile as we let ourselves out.

'God, she's gorgeous!' Anne said as we climbed back into the Land Rover.

'I've heard she's got five kids,' I remarked, starting

the engine. For a moment Anne almost believed me, but my straight face hid nothing and she slapped my hand playfully.

'Surely, not jealous?' she teased.

'She's married to a wrestler, apparently,' I continued.

'Oh yeah? What's she called, Mary?'

'No,' I said deadpan. 'Monica.'

As shopaholics we rounded off our glorious day by a trip to Sainsbury's giant superstore just outside Halifax. I spent fifty quid on a week's shopping and Anne insisted on buying food for what remained of the weekend.

Anne's mammoth overspending proved that, like me, she didn't want the weekend to end either. She spoilt and cossetted me, insisting I have a lie-in on Sunday morning as she saw to my chores.

Anne looked a bit battered when finally she returned to bed. She'd had a bit of a bust up with Erik who was a little jealous, but I soothed her pecked ankle and picked the straw out of her hair. Despite this, she lugged the telly upstairs and presented me with croissants and fresh coffee for breakfast.

Doris Day starred in *Pillow Talk*, the Sunday afternoon film. That weekend was better than a fortnight in Florida.

Chapter 16

Ten days later the cars started to arrive and it was during the chaos of delivery that I discovered Henrietta's, that champion layer, body.

Nestled on her favourite perch in a quiet corner of the chicken run, sat atop her last small brown egg, I knew immediately that her colourful feathery body was quite lifeless. I felt a moment's sadness, particularly for Erik who pecked fretfully at the chicken wire surrounding Henrietta's last home. Julia had accused me in the past of crediting the chicks with too much intelligence. Maybe I did, but Erik's distress was real enough, though I knew that should a good feed appear, his mourning would be short lived.

Wrapping the cooling body in newspaper, I left Henrietta in the outhouse. Despite the expense, I thought it wise to contact the local vet, Harry Barlow, and have him check out the cause of death. If some strange chicken disease had been responsible, I wanted to be prepared. Pure emotion prompted me to put her last brown egg under a nearby broody pullet in the hopes that it would hatch.

The reasons for her death weren't obvious. She'd not been set upon by foxes (they'd found richer pickings

outside the Kentucky take away in Halifax years ago).
We were seldom troubled by the wilder aspects of wild-
life anymore. She was unlikely to have been eggbound
either, the egg she'd died upon was proof of that. It
seemed old Henrietta had simply died. Chickens sometimes did that. One minute they were fighting, feeding
and fucking and the next they were just – dead. But
Harry would know for sure.

'Security's a bit heavy,' I said to Julia three days later.

We viewed the bottom fields as before from a raised
grassy platform whilst below us a breathtaking sight
unfolded. It was an extraordinarily beautiful early
autumn day and the sun, its power surely more suited
to a hot dry July, was reflected against gleaming
chrome, solid blacks and extravagant luscious reds, the
colours in fact, of money.

Only one car remained under wraps. Leisel's treas-
ured Mercedes had not yet seen daylight.

It had arrived the previous night, mysteriously under
the cover of darkness, and it remained in darkness still.
The delivery truck that had brought the car all the way
from South America, across the Atlantic and finally
from Folkestone to Calderton, was locked, bolted and
barred, safe from prying eyes and thieving hands. The
Custom's stickers were untouched and whole across the
lorry's back doors. A posse of strange looking men had
stayed with the vehicle throughout the night.

'I'm not sure about letting them stay on the farm,' I
complained to Julia. 'They look a bit rough to me.'

'They are a bit rough,' she said. 'That's the whole
point. Simone was particularly worried after she'd heard
about the break in at your house.' Julia looked thoughtfully at the culmination of her recent wheeling and
dealing. All the cars were securely clamped to their

temporary moorings and it would have taken a lot more than your average fourteen-year-old TWOCer to shift them. I doubted that even AnnaMaria could have stolen one.

'I suppose you're right,' I agreed somewhat reluctantly.

'Come on,' Julia said. 'Let's get some breakfast before the others arrive.'

The 'others' were Leisel and Simone. Julia had insisted they stay at the farm prior to the auction, though I didn't know what I could offer that the new Manchester Hilton couldn't. But again I'd reluctantly agreed to Julia's suggestion.

Calderton itself was awash with visitors. Occasionally a familiar face from the Town Hall dinner dance cropped up, and others, mostly men with exotic Eastern European accents, rubbed shoulders with the locals, some of whom had suddenly become landlords of bed and breakfast establishments.

Anne had regaled me with tales from George, my next door neighbour. Long retired and happy to mooch along until hypothermia or a stroke got him, he'd suddenly blossomed under the attention of a Ukraine couple. He, mysterious and overcoated, she the same, had arrived in a beautifully restored Trebant, that newly popular car that was successfully filling the tyre prints left by the 2CV. It was a shame it wasn't to be auctioned. The trendies of Todmorden would have snapped it up.

The two Ukrainians seemed happy to stay at George's run-down farm and pay a fortune for the privilege. 'Quaint,' they'd called it. 'Mugs,' George had confided to Anne. George was no fool. He'd hired a couple of the old girls from the village to do the cooking and cleaning while his 'guests' enjoyed their visit to his traditional 'Old English residence'. George in the meantime was down at the bookies, revelling in the sport of gentlemen. It was the first time in ten years he'd been able to splash out.

Suddenly Calderton was full of entrepreneurs who'd just been waiting for the right opportunity to make a killing. Some of them had waited seventy years!

Julia, like the village, was buzzing. I kept expecting her to rub her hands in glee. The auction was to be her personal financial saviour and she couldn't wait for it to get underway.

Simone's BMW and a hire car were parked outside the house when Julia and I returned. I sighed, knowing Leisel had been behind the wheel of the Hertz rental. The thought of being under the same roof as that unbearable and pretentious woman for any amount of time was almost more than I could bear.

We'd met only once since the dinner dance and the occasion had been spectacularly grim.

Julia, in an attempt to make us all jolly dykes together, had invited me, Anne and her niece for dinner at her swish place on the Quays. The thought of dinner on Julia had driven me there and with regards to Leisel, who thankfully would be arriving alone, I liked to think I'd give somebody the benefit of the doubt. AnnaMaria had declined with her customary sneer and a reluctant Anne had only agreed to come with me when I'd resorted to begging.

AnnaMaria had had the right idea.

Julia had insisted it would be a casual get-together, an occasion when we could meet and talk. I don't know what Julia had been reading, probably the A to Z of eighteenth-century lesbian etiquette.

And casual. Ha!

Never had a pair of jeans looked so out of place.

Leisel's ideas of casual clothing obviously bore no resemblance to mine. Her dress, 'Just an old thing I slop around in,' had only recently come off the Paris catwalk.

Julia, bless her, tried her utmost as the evening headed into a doomed and downward spiral.

Even Simone tried hard for the middle ground, but we were never destined to get on. At best it was obvious we would be grudging and very temporary business partners but the rarefied air surrounding Simone and particularly Leisel was not to my taste.

To be honest, the meal was the evening's saving grace.

As Anne and I struggled to make small talk with Julia's other guests, we were interrupted by the arrival of two Chinese gents *en route* from Chinatown.

Julia's big mahogany table was suddenly, inspirationally, transported to a Hong Kong setting. Lights were dimmed, candles were lit and a sumptuous table was set. Dim sum, noodles, vegetables I didn't recognise, rice, Peking duck and much else set off a pungent aroma that taste buds, unaffected by a clash of personalities, couldn't resist.

The two cooks left Julia's flat a couple of hundred pounds richer, while we devoured the banquet laid before us, and as we juggled with the intricacies of chopsticks and chop suey, we found we were too involved in the art of eating to talk. It was the only moment when we were all genuinely content.

Of course it couldn't last and as Julia cleared the table and laid out coffee we were forced to converse. In an attempt to steer the conversation clear of anything contentious, Anne dutifully admired Julia's rather splendid flat. But there's only so much you can say about the warm Sanderson paper that covered the walls or the strategically placed Pre-Raphaelite prints. Julia's flat always had an eighties feel to it, but she had found colours and paintings that suited her tastes and she was reluctant to change simply to follow fashion.

We were glad to leave at ten. My dislike of Leisel hadn't diminished and I'd remarked to Anne on the way home that I was relieved AnnaMaria hadn't been there to put her tuppence worth in. It had taken all the willpower I possessed not to make a few cracks myself. Things had got very prickly when we'd foolishly ventured into politics and the temptation to shove Leisel's right-wing ideology down her throat had been almost overwhelming.

'I don't know whether I can bear being near her,' I admitted to Julia.

'Well, at least she'll be on your territory this time,' Julia diplomatically took my side.

'I suppose I could always throw her out.'

Julia laughed as we approached the house. 'As long as it's after we've sold the Merc.'

The mystery car had been a topic of conversation that night.

'Is it really worth that much?' I asked Julia. 'I don't want to rain on your parade at this late stage but I thought the bottom had fallen out of the Classic's market.' I'd been reluctant to mention it, no doubt Julia knew more about such things than me, but a bloke on the car programme, *First Gear* had said as much the previous Wednesday.

'Depends who you're selling to,' Julia replied cryptically.

I let the subject drop. Julia's usually gobby mouth had gone tight and silent. It seemed there'd be nothing else forthcoming from her.

'Anyway,' she said after a moment, unable to stand the silence, 'I'm sure she's got other assets.'

'Oh?' I said, though it wasn't Leisel's assets I was concerned about.

'I'm sure her father took more than just a car to Colombia when he left Germany in '45.'

'Don't be so mysterious,' I said. 'What do you know?'

'I wish,' she mumbled. 'But let's face it, Leisel isn't what you'd call poor, is she? She does enough globe hopping after all. What was she telling us the other night? Next stop Russia? Not exactly Majorca, is it?'

I giggled. It was the first time I'd seen Julia this rattled for a long time. Julia's look stopped my laughter. 'Sorry,' I said. 'I know this is important to you. It's obviously just a game to Leisel.' I squeezed Julia's arm reassuringly. 'Perhaps some rich dyke's got more money than sense.'

'I hope somebody has,' Julia remarked quietly.

Chapter 17

The auction was scheduled for twelve. Up at my usual time, I left the livestock locked in their run. A thirty-minute running battle with Erik ensured that him and his pals wouldn't add to the panic-stricken confusion that existed elsewhere.

By mid-morning Calderton had descended on the farm.

Mrs Buckham, embracing the entrepreneurial spirit wholeheartedly, had bullied me by phone into letting her set up a 'Refreshment Centre' at the entrance to the farm. The last-minute call I'd received the previous night had been just short of hysterical and I figured I owed her one. I demanded a cut, of course, albeit a small one; her business sense would have been insulted otherwise.

From the vantage point of my bedroom window and with the aid of my powerful binoculars, I'd watched the visitors arrive. I'd spotted WPC Emma doing her policewomanly duties at the main road and I'm sure the abundance of guests that were obviously lesbian must have thrown her a bit.

Amongst this rich and rare breed mingled locals, whiz kids, rich kids and richer OAPs out for a bargain or a gossip. The international jet set were, however, aloof from the general mêlée. Perhaps the merriment was beneath them. I didn't know and cared less.

Julia had bucked up a bit from the night before, but perhaps that was because of Simone. I'd heard the bed springs creaking at three in the morning. And yes, I'd been jealous. I'd spent the night alone. Anne and I had made arrangements to see each other at the auction. A couple of nights without her was just two too many for me.

Julia was stressed and dressed to kill by nine and, as I devoured muesli, she smoked her way through breakfast. Simone had commandeered the bathroom and I'd last seen Leisel when I'd collected eggs at six. She'd not been seen since and that was fine with me.

'Do you want a cuppa?' I asked Julia, who was once more immersed in the finer details of auctioneering.

'Yes, no, whatever,' she mumbled, lighting a fresh cigarette from the butt of her old one. I took that as a 'yes' and placed a steaming mug in front of her.

'What time is it?' she asked for the fifth time.

'Half past,' I said, pinching a cigarette out of her packet. Though her mood had improved her nerves were catching, and I felt as though I'd break out in nervous eczema in sympathy.

'Half past what?' she asked, irritably tapping her untrustworthy watch face.

'Nine,' I replied, trying for calm.

'He's late, he said he'd be here for nine.'

'Who?' I asked through a stream of smoke. I stabbed the Gauloise into the ashtray. I couldn't afford to feel sick.

'Richard.'

'Simone's Richard?' I asked stupidly.

Julia rubbed her face wearily. 'He offered to be chief auctioneer.'

'Is that okay with you?' I interrupted, still doubtful of Simone's marriage of convenience story.

'I didn't have much choice,' she snapped. 'I can't afford to turn away a freebie, especially one with his sort of reputation. It would have cost a fortune to hire one.'

I pondered a moment as Julia shuffled papers.

'What the fuck is Simone doing?' she mumbled, as the sounds of splashing gained intensity upstairs. I didn't respond, just did my wifely duties and cleared away Julia's untouched cup and emptied the ashtray. Through the kitchen window I could see more punters arriving. Their cars were parked on an adjoining field. Another of Simone's ideas, she'd decided to charge a parking fee for each vehicle. She reckoned every pound counted. I bet the tax man did as well.

'I've got a confession to make,' Julia said suddenly.

'Oh?' Surprised, I turned from the kitchen window. In all the years I'd known her, through all her dodgy dealings and extra-marital affairs, she'd never confessed to anything. The Witch Finder General would have been hard pressed to obtain information from her.

The well-shuffled auction papers were stuffed untidily into her leather briefcase and Julia finger-brushed her newly cut black hair. 'It's about Caroline,' she said.

I waited for her to continue, pleased to note that I'd not given the woman a thought for days.

'Well, it's Leisel's fault, really,' she rambled. 'She's invited her here to the auction.' Julia paused, then added quietly, 'She's invited her to the party later as well.'

'What about Jocelyn, she won't like having her nose

pushed out will she?' The intricacies of lesbian courtship!

'Don't worry about her, she'll be doing the books all day.'

'You still haven't told me how all this came about, come on, dish the dirt, girl!'

Julia laughed. 'All I know is, Caroline met Jocelyn when she was doing some business with Richard.'

'What business?' I asked more intrigued than ever.

'I don't know, some car deal. Simone doesn't tell me everything you know. Anyway,' she said changing the subject, 'you don't mind about the party then?'

I shrugged, I wasn't sure what she wanted me to say. The party, to be held immediately after the auction, should have been for close friends only and the odd neighbour. I would have preferred to have the shindig in the marquee but Leisel had scuppered that idea. Apparently it wouldn't be ready in time for the 'do', whatever that meant. So rather than argue the toss I decided to throw a more intimate party at the farmhouse.

As my mind wandered Julia looked more uncomfortable by the minute. 'Will Anne mind?' she asked lamely.

I laughed aloud. 'There are that many people at the auction already chances are she won't even see her. Anyway, it sounds as though Caroline's already got her hands full.' I paused, suddenly rather shy. Glancing at the floor I said, 'It's special, me and Anne, pasts don't matter anymore.'

The words were as unexecpted to me as they were to Julia. They were nevertheless quite true.

'That's brilliant!' Julia exploded, relieved to be out of the hot seat. 'Anyway, I told her not to invite her,' she continued loftily, suddenly on firmer ground. 'I've got enough on my plate, I didn't want you upsetting as well.'

Julia's concern was astonishing. I had to laugh though, the scenario was as complicated as only lesbians can make it.

'Well, Julia, we're all grown ups. What's the worst that can happen? A row, a fall out? I'm sure we'll cope.' Magnanimous to the end, I caught Julia's eye and grinned.

It was a pity we didn't realise just how bad things could get.

Simone breezed into the kitchen ten minutes later, power dressed to her usual high standards. 'Morning,' she greeted us and reached elegantly for the teapot, which was empty. Someone suddenly rapped on the door and Simone, abandoning her breakfast, did the honours. A flustered skinhead staggered over the step.

'Simone, sweetheart,' the skinhead gasped, 'I'm so sorry I'm late, the damned bike wouldn't start.'

Top to toe in black leather, he squeaked rustily as he turned to survey the room, and me.

Slim, handsome, thirtysomething and very gay, the young man stepped lightly towards me, hand outstretched. 'Letty, I presume?'

'Richard, by any chance?' I asked and firmly shook his studded leather paw. He smiled and dimples appeared fetchingly across his narrow face. 'Any chance of a cuppa?' he asked. The barest trace of Scandinavian graced his accent. I threw a couple of tea bags into the pot and stuck the kettle on the Aga.

'Beautiful wood,' he said, indicating the wall-to-wall pine. 'Reminds me of home.' He was a real old charmer, it was unlikely he ever had a cold and lonely night.

'So,' he said, groping for the zip fastener at his throat.

'What are we up to?' With one fluid movement he unzipped his all-in-one leather outfit to reveal an expensive example of a grey Armani suit, saved from a funereal quality by the flash of a red waistcoat. Fascinated, I watched him step out of his leathers. Simone took his arm and guided him to the table.

A long conversation followed between the three of them. Costs were discussed, facts and projected figures that I had no interest in were bandied about. Julia tried to involve me in the planning but a red glaze of boredom eventually drove me out. That, and the thought of Anne already en route to the auction.

'I'm off,' I said to no one in particular.

Richard was on his feet in an instant. 'Aren't you coming with us?' A look of concern spread across his face.

'It's okay,' I smiled. I couldn't help but like him. 'I'll see you there.'

'Okay,' Julia murmured, too engrossed to look up. I could understand her change of attitude to Richard now I'd met him. A pink-and-gay cloud billowed around him, as threatening to Julia and Simone as a wet weekend in Skegness.

'Bye,' Simone called. I waved to the odd threesome and let myself out to the sunny, exciting day that lay ahead.

Chapter 18

Like Simone I'd dressed carefully that morning. Chicken-shitted jeans just wouldn't do, and I'd opted for the suit I'd last worn to the Town Hall. A bit over-dressed but I fitted in with the slightly unreal surroundings. I even decided to drive down to the auction and suddenly childishly excited by events, I ran to the shed to retrieve the 2CV. She'd not been used for a week or so and I was delighted when she started first time. Erik glared at my tricky manoeuvring and as I backed out carefully Julia flagged me down before I could set off.

'And where are you going?' she asked cheerfully, leaning against the driver's door.

'I'm leaving you mad makers of money to it. Any more of these financial and emotional shenanigans and my head will spin off. Anyway, I want to meet Anne.'

Laughing Julia nipped round to the passenger door and jumped in beside me. 'Drive on and don't spare the horses,' she yelled.

I slammed my foot to the floor and in response Miranda promptly stalled. Julia howled. 'All right then drive on and don't spare the donkeys!'

'Shut it,' I growled. 'Or you walk. Anyway, what

improved your mood? Ten minutes ago I thought you were going to have a nervous breakdown.'

Excitedly she grabbed my knee and gave it a firm and rather painful squeeze. Reflexes thus successfully tested my foot shot off the accelerator and Miranda ground to a shuddering halt again.

'We've just had a call about the Merc.' Julia paused for effect and gave a little drum roll on the dashboard with well-manicured fingers.

'And?' I encouraged as I restarted the engine.

'And,' she emphasised grinning, 'a private investor has shown considerable interest.'

I got the drum roll again. 'And what does that mean exactly?'

'It means, my little pumpkin, that the reserved price of seventy big ones is very likely to be smashed, mangled, scattered to the four winds.'

Her Italian heritage came screaming to the fore as she gesticulated wildly.

'Who is this idiot, I mean customer?' I enquired.

'Sorry,' Julia tapped her nose conspiratorially. 'Auctioneer's secrets. You'll just have to wait and see.' She turned to look at me as I swung the car off the driveway and joined the trickle of traffic already on the farm road.

'Aren't you excited, just a bit?' Julia pressed.

'Should I be?' I countered. Though of course I was. This was an event with a capital 'E'. But Julia's demands for my enthusiasm were so typical of her, I felt I had to challenge them, and then something in her expression made me relent. It was amazing to think that she had any success in business, her inner feelings were etched on her face for all to see.

'Of course I'm excited,' I confessed. 'I've not felt like this since . . .' I paused. I wanted to say 'since I met

Anne' but I didn't want to hurt Julia's feelings. She was not only guileless sometimes, but could be very sensitive too. So I added, 'Since the Pride March we went on, God, four years ago.' The speedy passage of time always threw me.

'That was wild wasn't it?' Julia reminisced. 'That's when I first met Simone.'

'I thought you'd only known her about six months?'

'I'd forgotten,' Julia smiled.

'How the hell could you forget someone like that?' Though Julia's forgetfulness was legendary, Simone was not a woman you forgot.

'Well, you don't remember her,' she challenged.

I laughed. 'Well, at least I don't think I do.' I paused for thought. Julia and I had been so pissed it was a wonder either of us could remember our own name, never mind a casual acquaintance. 'Simone remembered you though?'

'Apparently I made a lasting impression,' Julia smirked.

'You can tell me the whole story tonight over a drink,' I demanded.

I slowed to let a group of locals on foot pass by. George from next door tapped on the window and gave a little wave. I returned his wave and absently studied his companions. An impression of underplayed wealth surrounded the two Ukrainians. Their simple yet expensive gear suggested that not everyone was poor in the new East.

The field designated as the temporary car park drew near but Julia hastily switched off the indicator before I had a chance to take a left.

'Come on, Letty,' she scolded. 'Park nearer the marquee. It is your land, you can park where you damn well please.'

'Lazy sod,' I muttered, but followed her advice and the growing crowds to the auction area.

We got admiring glances as we parked next to a platform displaying a 1963 Aston Martin. I was tempted to put a price tag on Miranda, but sometimes it's enough just to make an entrance.

Chapter 19

Predictably, Julia dumped me immediately and made for the marquee and I was left to my own devices.

I searched in vain for a sign of Anne. I'd seen the library van parked up and I knew she was here somewhere. The crowds seemed to be converging at some point at the centre of the field and, lemming-like, I followed.

AnnaMaria's unmistakable voice carried above all others. A small knot of excitement gathered in my stomach, for wherever AnnaMaria was, Anne was sure to follow. I was right, but the scenario I stumbled across wasn't quite what I expected.

'How are we supposed to know what the fuss is all about if we can't have a proper look?' AnnaMaria bellowed as I edged my way through the spectators. In overalls and typical stance, AnnaMaria, jaw set, blonde crewcut singling her out from all the rest, leaned across the wooden fence that separated the crowds from the rather awesome vehicle that lay beyond.

A Mafia type, guarding the unveiled Silver Mercedes, threatened her wordlessly with a look. Before I could interfere a hand pulled gently at the sleeve of my jacket. Anne's heartening face smiled into mine and the knot in my stomach gave a final jolt before melting into a warm and wonderful glow. I was speechless for a moment as Anne dragged me away from the spectacle.

'What's going on?' I managed as Anne brazenly tucked her arm through mine.

'They won't let her look at the car,' she confided and mischievously she pulled me to her and kissed my cheek. 'You look lovely,' she whispered. 'I've missed you.' I clutched at her fingers, fuck the neighbours. Anyway I knew they all watched *Emmerdale* so welcome to the nineties.

'I wanted you to come over last night, but there was no room at the inn,' I explained. 'What with Simone, Leisel and Julia, and then Richard turned up this morning.'

'He's doing the actual auctioneering, isn't he?' Anne asked as she slipped her arm from mine and opened her shoulder bag.

'You're very well informed, Madam,' I mused, laughing.

Anne waved a glossy pamphlet in my face. 'You should read your own advertisements,' she mock scolded. 'Fifteen quid this bloody thing cost.'

I prised the outrageously priced article from her hands. It was an updated version of the programme I'd received a few weeks earlier. Richard graced the cover, together with a flattering picture of the farm and a stunning photo of the Mercedes. The car, complete with running board, red leather seats and minus its convertible top, presented itself as a remarkable machine, I had to admit. But seventy grand's worth? I doubted it.

'It's a ridiculous price,' Anne commented, reading over my shoulder.

'The pamphlet or the car?' I laughed.

'Both! But Richard doesn't quite look like I imagined.'

The photo made him seem much butcher than he actually was. 'He's not a bit like that,' I admitted. 'More Torvil than Dean if you get my drift.'

'Must run in the family,' Anne muttered, harking back to her first, mixed, impression of Simone. It was the nearest I'd heard her come to a nasty remark. 'Anyway let's rescue AnnaMaria before she gets in a fight.' The rumbles in the background had got ominously loud.

'I'll have a word with Julia after the auction. Perhaps she'll let AnnaMaria have a closer look at the car then.'

And with that we dragged a grumbling AnnaMaria away.

An hour later the multitudes were being cleverly worked into a frenzy of spending, whether they could afford it or not. Richard, seemingly everywhere at once, flattered, cajoled and persuaded the crowds to reach for their wallets. He was an expert at this, I could tell at a glance. Like a high-class market trader.

Even George, the miserly old git, parted with a long-hidden wad of money in exchange for a 1965 Bedford Van that he had absolutely no need for and would probably write off within the week. I suspected he was trying to impress the Ukrainian couple. They probably thought he was just soft in the head. But he seemed happy enough and he enthused over it to anyone who would listen. The Eastern pair wandered off, bored.

All this was just an aside for the real thing and as host I demanded a front row seat in the marquee for me and my guests as the hammer fell for the penultimate time.

The stage was set for an extraordinary event. Lesser vehicles had exchanged hands for inflated prices, due

152

as much to Richard's expertise as to the vehicles themselves, and my gloomy predictions concerning the slump in the Classic Car market were being proved entirely wrong.

Richard took his place at the podium and didn't look in the least fazed by two hours of non-stop talking, selling and probably lying through his teeth.

Anne sat quietly by my side as, fascinated, we looked on. AnnaMaria fidgeted, only slightly mollified by my offer to persuade Julia to show her the auction's star later in the day.

Julia sat with Simone and Jocelyn at the back of the stage doing sums on a laptop. Leisel had effectively disappeared.

The audience quieted, only the murmur of voices speaking into mobile phones disturbed the peace.

'Ladies and Gentlemen,' Richard began, his deceptively soft voice reaching into all corners of the arena. 'We've all had a long day,' he acknowledged. Voices whispered and heads nodded in agreement. 'So I won't waste anyone's time.' Suddenly aggressive, he had everyone's attention. 'You've all seen it, and we all know what a rarity is on sale today. I won't go into precise specifications, your catalogue will detail all that. The one thing it can't explain is the sheer majesty that comes with experiencing the car in its full glory. I have driven many, many vehicles,' he intoned, his voice gathering momentum, 'but none with quite its character, quite its charisma, nor indeed quite its history.' He paused. It was like watching Richard Burton doing Henry V, but more so. The audience were hooked.

'When I tested the car at three this morning . . .' I glanced at Anne and she pulled a face. An obvious lie, the car had been under wraps up to a couple of hours ago and Julia had assured me it had not been driven for twenty years.

Richard went on, unchallenged, 'I was taken with its sheer grace and its ability to turn heads.'

Even if it had been true the only heads that would have turned at that hour of the morning would have been countless sheep grazing on the moors.

'Should I have been fortunate enough, or wealthy enough, I would have parted with the seventy thousand pounds reserve price there and then.'

The crowd gasped, not everyone had forked out fifteen quid for a catalogue.

Richard slammed his gavel on the podium and the stunned crowds settled down. The mobiles took up their mutterings in tongues unknown to me.

'So, who will start the proceedings?' Richard asked.

A hand shot up and we all craned our necks to see who had seventy thousand pounds to throw away. An ordinary woman in her late fifties clutching a pencil and visibly sweating had been the first to bite.

That first offer, as Julia had confidently predicted, was smashed at the first hurdle.

Within ten minutes we were into six figures. The bidding slowed as the impossible price of £120,000 was reached, Richard looked as though he was preparing to call it a day. Once, twice, the gavel descended.

'One fifty,' a voice called from the back.

A shocked silence descended. Richard feigned surprise. I looked around, trying to locate the bidder. The man from the Ukraine, leaning uninterestedly against a post, had spoken.

A mobile, gabbing rapidly, pushed the price up a further ten thousand, but a leisurely, 'Two hundred,' from the well-dressed Eastern European, was decisive.

154

It was done. Wood crashed against wood as Richard pronounced 'Sold.'

Incredibly, a car worth a fraction of its starting price had gone for just short of a quarter of a million pounds. If I hadn't been there to see it, I would never have believed it.

'I doubt if you'll get to look at it now,' I muttered to a stunned AnnaMaria as we shuffled out of the marquee.

She didn't comment and in retrospect that should have been warning enough.

The crowds dispersed much quicker than they had arrived, probably encouraged by George's Kamikaze driving as anything else. He left the field in his new acquisition in a cloud of exhaust fumes and flying soil.

Leisel made a sudden appearance, no doubt drawn by the smell of money, and I passed her huddled in a corner by the marquee with the new owners of the Mercedes.

To avert a sense of anti-climax, I invited Anne and her niece back to the house where all was quiet and peaceful, at least for the time being.

'It wasn't worth it, you know?' AnnaMaria insisted as we climbed into Miranda for the short journey home. 'More money than sense some folk. I bet even George got a better deal,' she continued, as we followed George's smoky progress through the farm.

'If he doesn't plough into the barn first,' Anne said, smiling at the thought of George as a bargain hunter.

She lightly draped her hand on my leg and all else was forgotten in a sudden surge of lust. Anne gazed through the windscreen, a slight smile on her lips. The little hussy knew exactly what she was doing.

I drove the car back to the house where a little red Suzuki moped graced the driveway.

'Do you like her?' AnnaMaria enquired before I had a chance to comment.

'It's great,' I enthused. 'New?'

'To me. Been around the clock a few times but it gets me about. I was sick of buses. It'll do while I save up for a car. Anyway, I'm off,' she said leaping from the car. 'I'll be back later for the party, if that's okay. I'll see if I can persuade Andy along. He had a pool match today, if he's not through to the finals he'll probably come.'

'Fine,' I said, remembering suddenly that I'd have to warn Anne of Caroline's intentions. Somehow we'd managed to give her the slip at the auction.

AnnaMaria pulled on a black crash helmet and started her bike. Its 'phut phut' could be heard for miles. I let Anne into the deserted house. 'God,' I said, 'I've got to get into the shower, I've been up for hours and I feel filthy.'

'Come on, then,' Anne said, grabbing my hand. 'I'll scrub your back.'

I was beginning to think Anne had some sort of water fetish, not that I was complaining. The Aga-heated water was stone cold when, ages later, we re-emerged.

Chapter 20

'It's all right, you know?' Anne insisted for the umpteenth time that afternoon.

Over lunch I'd explained Caroline's forthcoming intentions. Mercifully Anne had laughed off my concerns and scolded me for my unfounded jealousy.

'To be honest, Leisel's welcome to her,' she said, clearing our plates away. 'It was my first experience, remember, and I was infatuated. Weren't you with yours?'

I nodded my head noncommittally. I'd been seventeen and truly madly passionately in lust with a friend of my mother's. But that's another story altogether.

Thankfully Anne didn't ask me to explain. 'Anyway, I'm over it, her,' Anne explained. 'She can't touch us.'

I dragged Anne back to the table at that point before domesticity overwhelmed her and she was tempted to do the washing up.

'Leave that,' I ordered. 'I'm expecting the caterers around any time, it won't kill them to wash a few more pots.'

Anne looked surprised. 'A bit extravagant,' she said.

'After today Julia can well afford it,' I quipped,

pulling Anne closer for a kiss. The phone's strident ringing interrupted our tête-à-tête.

Reluctantly I released Anne and went into the hall to answer the hideous thing.

'Letty, it's Harry Barlow from the veterinary surgery,' a male voice said. 'It's about the post mortem on the chicken.'

In the excitement of recent events I'd almost forgotten poor old Henrietta's demise. 'Sorry, Harry, I should have rung last week. What's the verdict? Nothing infectious I hope?' Not that the rest of the brood seemed affected.

'Well, strictly speaking, no.' He paused. 'But it's something I'd like to have a word with you about, privately, not over the phone.'

'Oh?' I said, puzzled.

'Look, I've got an hour free later today. I'll call round, if that's okay.'

'That's fine, though I'm having a bit of a do after today's auction, so it may be a bit chaotic.'

'I'll be round about seven then. Save me a sandwich, won't you? Bye.'

The phone went dead. Another mystery, though Harry did fancy himself as a crime writer after having a couple of short stories published. Comes with being a vet in Yorkshire, they all fancy themselves as the next James Herriot.

I dragged Anne out with me to check on the chickens though, after Harry's odd call. Healthy and sleepy, the brood were all conked out for the afternoon, only Erik showed any interest and he eyed Anne's ankles with relish. Warily she backed out of the chicken run before he had a chance to pounce. It was obvious they would never get on.

A little yellow ball of fluff shot between my feet,

kicking up sawdust in its wake. Erik whacked him spitefully as he zoomed past. It could only be Henrietta's chick, hatched at last so late in the season by its surrogate mother. After a short chase I picked it up for closer examination. A tricky manoeuvre followed, but after a moment I was sure it was a cockerel. Anne was thrilled, though it would probably grow into a noisy bossy little creature just like his dad. Erik's genes ran through the flock like a rash.

'So what will you call him?' Anne enquired after I'd returned him to his stepmum. I thought a moment. 'It'll have to be Henry I suppose, nearest I can get to Henrietta.'

Anne beamed. So Henry it was.

I left the chickens locked in the run, much to Erik's annoyance. It was strange, but if I'd ever had children I doubt if I'd have been half as protective.

The caterers arrived as promised and Anne and I pottered around the garden so as not to get under their feet. So many strangers had been in my house of late, I felt as though I were running a hotel. But not for long! I vowed that this was a once in a lifetime occasion. It was beginning to feel once too often already.

But there again, my period was due.

The party was entertainment for the most oddly assorted group of people ever likely to get together under one roof.

Julia arrived first, looking rich and relaxed, as stress free as I'd ever seen her. Surprising what a swelled bank account can do.

She was full of it, of course, and in between mouthfuls of nibbles that Patsy and Edina would have been proud of, she rabbited on about the auction's success. Only a few of the vehicles remained unsold and they would be whisked off to wherever they had come from first thing in the morning. The ones that had changed hands were busily being loaded onto trucks at that very moment *en route* for destinations far and wide.

The Mercedes, that over-priced rich man's plaything, would stay under guard on the farm overnight, awaiting shipment to the Ukraine the following day.

'Don't worry.' Julia said, between mouthfuls. 'Your field will be as pristine as it was before we arrived.'

'What about my nerves?' I joked.

'Nothing wrong with your nerves,' she snorted, and she delved again into the Japanese finger food.

'What exactly are you eating?' Anne enquired, looking suspiciously at the fishy assortment that littered my huge pine kitchen table. 'Has it stopped breathing?'

I giggled as Julia exhorted her to try it. I left them to their culinary discussion; other arriving guests were trying to knock the back door down.

Two hours later the house was packed and the food was disappearing fast. A strange mixture of music boomed from my elderly stereo. Ukrainian folk music followed Frank Sinatra. My REM contribution lasted only half a song, so I left the stereo and, strangely, George in charge of the tapes. Happy as a pig in shit, he'd brought several bottles of his own home-made beer and he seemed perfectly content nestled in front of the speakers, chatting happily to the sweaty woman who had made the first bid for the Mercedes.

Several of Julia's dykey friends had made an appearance, at least one had parted with some cash, but they seemed unwilling to mingle and instead took over the back room, a whiff of Polo drifting through the gaps in the door. I didn't blame them for not wanting to mix with the locals, it was hard enough to get a sensible conversation out of my neighbours at the best of times.

Mrs Buckham had made a short appearance, mainly to thank me for a wonderful, interesting and profitable day. She'd sold all her produce from her prime position on the gate and she was thrilled. Inevitably we talked eggs for a while and then she left, another satisfied customer.

Caroline was one of the last to arrive and one of the first to leave. 'Hi,' she said, breezing in alone as the party was in full swing. Gone were the untidy dreadlocks, a much more sophisticated woman greeted me now. Leisel's influence at a guess. I bristled inwardly but was outwardly polite. I was determined that this well-dressed woman would not get under my skin.

Smiling icily I said, 'No Leisel, then?'

'Oh, she's busy at the moment, finalising the deal. She said she may join me later.'

Not 'us' or 'the party' or 'Julia's guests'. Just 'me'. Perhaps I was being petty.

She slipped off her long, black, double-breasted linen jacket to reveal a skimpy low cut dress that was a far cry from the jeans and leather jacket that I'd been used to. From low-life to lipstick lezzy in one easy lesson I thought nastily.

She draped her coat across my unoffered arm. 'Is Anne around?' she asked smoothly.

'I'm here,' a voice said behind me. Anne returning from a trip to the loo smiled guardedly at her first and former lover.

'I'll go and hang your coat up,' I said hurriedly. 'Anne, I'll be in the lounge with Julia if you need me.'

Anne smiled warmly and only she saw me open the kitchen cupboard that served as the coat rack, and sling Caroline's flashy coat on the floor. Pettiness can be very satisfying.

161

Five minutes later Anne joined me and Julia in the lounge. I looked over her shoulder.

'Where is she?' I enquired, feigning unconcern.

'I told her to fuck off,' Anne said bluntly.

Julia choked on her wine. 'Really?' she gasped.

'Yes, really, I hope you didn't mind, Letty, but I think I frightened off one of your guests.' Anne's eyes sparkled with mischief.

I was delighted, if a little surprised. 'Fine with me, I can't stand her. If you see Leisel you can tell her the same, and Jocelyn come to that.'

Julia cackled at the thought.

'It's surprising how crumpled linen can get in just a few minutes,' Anne said dryly.

I smiled, a wickedness shared.

'Why did you tell her to clear off?' Julia was intrigued.

Anne slipped her hand in mine and clearly debated answering. When finally she did, I had reason to detest Caroline even more. 'She made a pass at me,' she confessed.

'My God, that woman's got some nerve,' Julia slurred. 'What happened to Jocelyn, eh? Couldn't keep out of each other's knickers up to yesterday.'

George, drunkenly preparing to leave with his new lady friend, stumbled as Julia's words registered. We silently watched the woman help him to his feet and drag him toward the back door. They crunched their way down the driveway waving drunkenly in our general direction. Obviously there was life in the old dog yet, or he'd taken a shine to her purse. Whatever.

Anne continued thoughtfully, 'They're non-monogamous, apparently.'

'Not half,' Julia observed merrily, 'some people are just never satisfied.' Pretty rich coming from her. We dwelt on these nuggets in silence for a moment. I felt relief more than anything, though Anne was still clearly annoyed.

'Sorry,' Julia said unsteadily. 'I feel responsible for her being here at all.' Suddenly she giggled, the buckets of wine she'd consumed were having the desired effect. 'I don't have to keep Leisel sweet now, do I?' Mischief lay etched on her handsome olive features.

'Wait till the cheque clears,' I advised. 'Do me a favour would you, Julia? See to the stereo, this music's driving me nuts.'

George had left Mantovani playing and a woman can only stand so much. She tottered off to put things right while I gave Anne a much needed hug.

Mantovani was replaced loudly by the Sounds of the Sixties. An improvement of sorts. A grinning Julia returned to bellow over the music that I had a visitor at the front door.

'Who?' I mouthed.

'Some bloke,' she bellowed back and returned to her job as DJ.

'I'll help Julia with the music,' Anne suggested. 'The sixties may have been my era but I was never a fan of Lulu.'

I went through the back door and followed the path round the house. Erik squawked and his newly hatched son peep-peeped in contest. He had a way to go before he could outshout his dad.

Local vet Harry Barlow stood on the drive examining AnnaMaria's new bike. I checked my watch, I couldn't believe it was already seven.

'Harry,' I called. 'Do you want to come in?'

'No, it's okay, Letty. I've got a call out so I won't be able to stay long.'

Harry was a tall man, maybe six feet three, though the width of his rugby playing shoulders made him look

163

smaller. His size also commanded a lot of respect for, at only twenty-eight, not many of the local farmers would have taken him seriously without it. Big-framed and good natured he was the sort of man my mother would have loved me to marry.

Fat chance.

'It was an odd phone call, Harry,' I said, standing in his shadow. 'What's the mystery?'

He rubbed his square jaw and whiskers rasped against skin. 'I'm not sure how to say this, Letty,' he began. 'It's a bit peculiar, to say the least.'

'What is it?' I pressed. A horrible feeling of dread was creeping up around me. 'The other hens seem to be all right. In fact we've got a newcomer.'

'Well,' he hedged, 'the others should be all right, providing they haven't eaten the same as the one that died.'

'She wasn't poisoned, was she?' I asked in horror. A thousand images leapt into my mind. My recent break in was just one of them.

'In a manner of speaking, yes. That's why I wanted to speak to you on your own. It's not something you'd want to broadcast. I thought about going to the police but decided to see you first,' he droned.

'Harry! What, for God's sake?'

'Your hen,' he explained clearing his throat nervously. 'I found traces of cocaine in her bloodstream.'

Chapter 21

I hurried back to the house as Harry took his leave with promises to keep the information under wraps. Cocaine poisoning only spelt one thing to me. Leisel. I'd not forgotten her fondness for the stuff at the Town Hall. The fact that she, or someone she knew, had brought it into my house made me seethe. I didn't know how Henrietta had got her beak on some, but I'd wring the information out of Leisel one way or the other. It dawned on me suddenly who the culprit could be. I don't know how I'd missed it up to now. Gauloise smoking, woman who knew Leisel? There was only one person; and that was Jocelyn. But why would she want to break into my house, what was the point?

Tormented I beckoned Anne upstairs and in private I told her the disturbing news.

'AnnaMaria was right then, about Leisel's habit,' she commented, equally upset by the vet's report. 'But what is Jocelyn up to, how is she involved?'

I shrugged, confused. 'Where is AnnaMaria anyway?' I asked. 'Her bike's outside.'

Anne looked through the bedroom window. 'Oh, she'll not be far away. You know what she's like. What will you do about Leisel?'

'I'm going to give her this for starters,' I said, waving Harry's sixty-pound bill in the air.

'You could report it, I suppose,' Anne suggested as we sat on the bed. 'You could tell WPC Emma whatsername. She's a dyke, she might listen without dropping your name in it. Maybe make a few enquiries . . .' she finished lamely, recognising the unlikelihood of this.

'Yeah,' I agreed dryly. 'The case of the Murdered Chicken.'

It was an impossible situation. Damned if you do and damned if you don't.

'No, I don't think so. I'll just have to tackle Leisel later. It's one thing poisoning yourself but quite another when I get drawn into it. Makes you sick. All that money just to shove it up your nose.' I took a deep breath to calm myself down. 'Oh well, there's nothing I can do about it now. Let's go and join the party, a few drinks might help.'

We trundled downstairs and helped ourselves to much-needed alcohol.

Three bottles of Diamond White and I wasn't quite so ready to behead Leisel on sight.

Julia herded the party goers together. 'Simone just rang, she's gone to the pub, are you two coming?'

'Will Leisel be there?' I asked carefully.

'I doubt it, she's busy cracking champagne open with the two Ukrainians in the marquee at the moment. Oh, come on, Letty. Anne, try and persuade her, there's bound to be a lock in and we're running out of booze fast.'

'Anne, you go with her if you want. I'm going to see Leisel before I go completely off the boil.'

'Why, what's up?' Julia enquired, looking puzzled.

'I'll explain later,' Anne interrupted. 'And no, Letty,

I won't let you tackle her on your own. Julia, you haven't seen AnnaMaria and Andy lately have you?'

'Briefly,' Julia replied, retrieving her coat from the kitchen cupboard. 'Well, AnnaMaria anyway. She came in when you were upstairs. Took one look at the food and cleared off. She's probably gone to the pub too, rowing with Simone at this very moment I shouldn't wonder.'

'Julia,' a designer dyke, resplendent in suit and Fedora, called. 'Let's get going, the pub will be closing before long.'

Julia flashed her a charming smile. 'I doubt it,' she murmured. But nevertheless she made for the door and like a modern-day Pied Piper led her flock out, public house bound. I was very tempted to go along, if just to see the local reaction.

But I resisted and Anne and I were left alone.

It was totally dark by the time we left the house. A round and yellow moon lit our way, and the lights from the marquee beckoned in the distance.

'If I don't say something now, I never will,' I explained to Anne, as we walked quickly through the farm. The night air was chilly and we'd both donned coats over our finery.

'I do understand,' Anne said smiling and tucking her arm in mine. 'But Leisel seems a bit unpredictable, so don't go upsetting yourself if she tries to call your bluff.'

'Yeah, but money talks with her sort, doesn't it? I know it doesn't seem much, one dead chicken, but the fact that she can leave cocaine just lying around really does my head in.'

'I know,' Anne soothed. 'If AnnaMaria finds out, she'll kill her.'

There were signs of activity as we neared the auction

area. Most of the cars had gone by then, only one or two remained. I could see the Ukrainian's Trebant parked by the side of the Merc, its economic lines dwarfed by its classy German cousin. The truck that had delivered the Mercedes was slowly being reversed.

I stopped in my tracks, confused when one of Leisel's guards climbed into the Trebant and drove it up a ramp into the back of the spacious van.

'I didn't think they were selling the Trebant,' I muttered to Anne.

'Maybe it's part of the deal,' she replied and, laughing, added, 'I suppose Leisel's got to drive something. Hell of a swap though.'

The van doors were locked, bolted and secured as we moved closer, watching the odd proceedings. Voices drifted through the still night air. Leisel's came over loud and clear, 'So what do you suggest we do with her?' she snapped to someone I couldn't see. Hardly the champagne popping I'd been expecting.

' "We" doesn't come into it,' a male voice snapped back, Richard by the sound of it. 'It's what *you* two do that matters. I've done my share. I'm out of here. I've got a plane to catch and if I were you I'd be doing the same.'

'I can't, can I?' she growled. 'I've got to get the Trebant out of the country. I can't let these buffoons do it.'

Anne gripped my arm more forcibly. 'I don't think now's a good time, ' she suggested quietly.

'I know,' I agreed. 'But I'm curious, aren't you?' Something about Leisel's tone made me want to know more. 'Come on, Anne. Let's see what she's up to.' I stifled nervous giggles and, sighing, Anne nodded.

We were already skirting the field by the time we heard more. This time the words were hissed angrily in a language other than English. Anne nervously pulled her coat tighter and with a worried look, grabbed my arm and pulled me behind a hawthorn bush that had been allowed to grow wild on the uncultivated field. Apparently she had understood them, even if I hadn't.

'What's she saying?' I hissed in surprise. In response Anne clamped her hand across my mouth and urgently pressed a silencing finger across her own lips.

Leisel droned on, gabbled words rising and falling in a language I didn't know. Anne's eyes widened in shock.

Suddenly the van carrying the Trebant roared into life.

'We've got to go back,' Anne insisted, desperately pulling me to my feet. 'And ring the police.'

'What? What's she saying?' I demanded sensing the panic in my lover.

'It's not just cocaine,' Anne's voice cracked in shock. 'They're talking about plutonium!' Her voice hit another octave. 'Don't you see?' she demanded, hauling me backwards. 'They're exchanging drugs for weapons. Plutonium. A fucking nuclear bomb!'

Chapter 22

We were too late. The van carrying the Trebant was already moving. Its headlights, picking out every shadow, pinned us to our spot behind the hawthorn bush. It pulled to a halt just past the marquee, though its powerful engine continued to rumble. Anyone happening to glance in our direction would spot us immediately if we attempted to flee.

My heart hammered in time to the engine as Anne, with a knowledge of the German Leisel and Richard had used, explained the gist of the shouted conversation.

'It's happening all the time,' she explained into my ear. 'You must have read about gun and drug exchanges, especially since things changed so much in Europe.'

'But where's it going?' I asked naively.

'The drugs to Eastern Europe and the plutonium to South America.'

'My God,' I stammered. 'You don't expect it to happen in Yorkshire, especially on my farm.' I could feel a confused ramble coming on. 'But how did they get through customs?' My naivety knew no bounds.

'I don't know,' my sleuth admitted. 'I couldn't hear anything else.'

Suddenly the van's engine died, though its lights continued to illuminate the countryside. Somehow events took an even further downward swing and the sickening sound of flesh on flesh was followed an an unearthly scream. The screams turned to moans. Anne was ashen.

'AnnaMaria!' she breathed. She gripped my wrist painfully. 'Letty, that was AnnaMaria. Oh my God!' All purposefulness had left her and she sat down, a whoosh of breath escaping her.

The screams, while horrible, could have been from anybody. 'Are you sure?' I asked, taking in her illuminated features. I secretly hoped it was one of the drug traffickers, caught with her nose in a bag.

'She screamed like that when her mother died,' she replied softly.

I had no idea as to what to do. This chicken farmer was way out of her league. I risked a glance through the prickly thorns of the hawthorn bush. Leisel, clearly visible in the van's lights, was gesticulating wildly at one of the men who had been guarding the Mercedes. Hurriedly he retrieved a can from the van's cab and disappeared from sight around the back of the marquee. I had a sudden terrible insight into his intentions.

Movements from the camp had taken on an air of finality. Richard finally made an appearance and he leapt hastily into the Mercedes. The chug-chug of a protesting engine echoed around the field as he tried in vain to start it. But for all its engineering, it wouldn't budge. Flustered, he retrieved a crank from the boot and, bypassing the electrical systems, started the slow process of hand-cranking the engine. In the distance, at the rear of the marquee, my suspicions took shape as the first lazy spirals of flame drifted into the sky.

'Come on, Anne, quick,' I said as a wild idea took shape, and I dragged Anne to her feet. She moaned when she saw the flames. 'AnnaMaria, dear God, AnnaMaria.'

Instead of heading for the marquee as I think Anne expected, I ran with her, hand in hand, stumbling over the uneven surface toward the side field that had served as the car park. There, just a hundred yards away was, as I'd hoped, Anne's library van.

'Keys, keys, have you got your keys?' I gasped as the treacherous path took my breath. Anne lurched along by my side. 'They're in the van,' she managed as we took those last hundred yards at a staggering gallop.

We reached it just as the lorry carrying the Trebant hurtled up the road. Four figures were crammed in the cab, two of them instantly recognisable, Jocelyn and Caroline. Mercifully, they were too preoccupied to notice me and Anne clambering into the pride of West Yorkshire's library services.

The keys were in the ignition and the engine burst into life at the first turn. I'd taken the decision to drive, Anne was incapable and though I'd never driven anything remotely like it before, I figured it wouldn't be that difficult.

How wrong can you be?

Filled with the infamous donkey juice, the vehicle bucked, chugged and complained as I grappled with the unfamiliar and complicated gears.

Sweating and cursing loudly and with screamed instructions from Anne, I finally swung the van in the right direction. The vehicle yawed right to left and the engine complained loudly at the demands I made on it. Finally, in third gear and on a slight slope, the marquee grew larger in my sights.

We crashed through thickets and over paths that had

172

never been designed for this sort of treatment. Maniacally I added the field's destruction to the growing list of demands I would make on Leisel. I didn't dare think of AnnaMaria, though Anne intoned her name over and over again.

My headlights picked out a panicking Richard and whilst I made no deliberate decision to plough into him, it was only luck and instinct that saved him from the library van's wheels. The stationary Mercedes had no such option and, with a sickening crunch, the front of the car disintegrated in a cacophony of wrenching metal and screeching brakes. The ruined car shuddered backwards for ten yards before ploughing into a strut supporting the tent. The boot popped open and a cloud of white powder exploded into the air.

Anne, her former panic and distress replaced by pure anger and a protective need that I could only guess at, was out of the van in seconds. Her only desire was to find and protect her niece.

As I struggled with my jammed door I saw Anne grab a dazed Richard and deliver a Glasgow kiss that Rab C Nesbitt would have been proud of. Poleaxed, he hit the floor and a desperate Anne disappeared into a maelstrom of burning material and crackling supports that had once been the marquee.

My instincts were less well honed and a strong hand hoisted me from my seat and flung me to the floor. Muttering in German, Leisel stomped on my face. Pain exploded and all I could do was roll away from her merciless foot. Blood trickled from my throbbing and probably broken nose as I scrabbled under the front of the cooling library van.

Sobbing and relentless in defeat, Leisel jabbed me with a length of metal. Pain again as the sharp metal gouged my legs, my arms and my unprotected head.

173

The jabbing suddenly stopped just as the fear of losing my eyes became very real, and from my vantage point I watched as Leisel hit the floor. A very singed AnnaMaria lay atop her, punching wildly.

I rolled painfully from my hiding place and was astonished at the scene. Anne dragged her niece from Leisel's still but breathing form as Julia desperately tried to stop Simone doing her husband some serious bodily harm.

Julia spotted me and obviously decided he wasn't worth saving and left them to it.

'I saw the flames,' Julia gasped. 'The fire engine will be here in a minute. What the hell happened? My God, look at your face.'

'I don't want to, thanks,' I managed, through my burst nose. Grateful to Julia though I was, I gently pushed her to one side and limped toward my sobbing lover and her niece.

'Christ, just look at you,' Anne said through her tears. 'And your suit, it's ruined.'

I hugged them both. 'That's something else the bitch owes me,' I managed before darkness and the soft earth engulfed me.

Chapter 23

Everything mends of course, including my broken nose.
All that's left of the bizarre chain of events is a huge
scorch mark on the bottom field.

The immediate enquiry passed me by somewhat as I
spent a dazed couple of days in the hospital.

The police were back and forth with all sorts of
questions. Most of them repeated at least twice. WPC
Emma was my personal guard for a while, for which I
was grateful, and she managed to keep CID and God
knows who else at a firm arm's length.

Anne was constantly by my side and alternated her
visits between AnnaMaria, who'd sustained some nasty
burns, and me. I got most of the story from her.

She'd been right about the drugs conspiracy. It had
taken the police days to retrieve the cocaine from the
bottom field. Some had been blown away and was scattered to the four winds, never to be retrieved. A small
amount had been caught in the fire, but most of it was
hidden throughout the Mercedes' expensive fittings. A
scam of some complexity, the drugs had been destined
to wind up somewhere in Russia, with Jocelyn as chief
negotiator. (I got that from Julia so I wouldn't take it
as gospel.)

Tests were done by the army on my field for signs of contamination but thankfully all was clear. We didn't need another Chernobyl in Yorkshire. The Trebant, with its deadly cargo, was found abandoned at Folkestone and Jocelyn and the Ukrainians are still wandering the countryside somewhere. The police seem pretty confident that they'll be picked up, though the police always are.

Richard recovered from his wife's attack and though Simone was suspected of involvement for awhile, she never had to join him and Leisel in prison awaiting trial.

It's odd – I expected everything to be tied up neatly, but real life, unlike the lesbian PI stories that I love so much, just isn't like that. Caroline who, everybody is agreed, was involved somewhere down the line has disappeared, but I'm sure if she ever makes an appearance she'll be charged too. Nice thought anyway.

As a conspiracy theorist I can be forgiven for assuming everything was meticulously planned; my farm used for the perfect set up, my friends duped along with me but all that would put Simone firmly under suspicion and as far as I know she's not. Also . . . well, I could go on but you don't need my explanations. You can read about the trial yourself. If the national press don't cover it, the *Calderton Echo* certainly will.

The locals are looking forward to the trial, which is scheduled for June and, as a summer spectator sport, it will beat Wimbledon hands down. Mrs Buckham's already booked daily coach trips to and from Leeds Assizes. Perhaps she could flog a few sandwiches during the interval.

There's just a bit of news to round things off. As soon as we'd got our wits about us, Anne agreed to move in with me. AnnaMaria did too, which makes life jolly interesting. She still sees Andy, who played the doting boyfriend for a while, and surprisingly, despite the fact that her nosiness nearly got her killed, is still interested in classic cars. So I gave them Miranda, my 2CV to play with.

Me and Anne were heroes for a while: 'DRUG BUSTING FARMER AND LIBRARIAN CRACK INTERNATIONAL CONSPIRACY' was one rather extravagant headline, but six months down the line it's old news.

We got a letter from Julia today. She's gone back to live in Italy. Sensibly, Simone went with her, though they'll both have to come back for the trial. They want to know if they can borrow the 2CV, some Classic Car convention over there, so I've passed the request on to AnnaMaria.

It's spring again and everything is blossoming, including the chickens. I'd better go and feed them, otherwise there'll be no peace. And then bed. I wonder if Anne fancies an early night?

Established in 1978, The Women's Press publishes high-quality fiction and non-fiction from outstanding women writers worldwide. Our list spans literary fiction, crime thrillers, biography and autobiography, health, women's studies, literary criticism, mind body spirit, the arts and the Livewire Books series for young women.
Our bestselling annual *Women Artists Diary* features the best in contemporary women's art.

The Women's Press also runs a book club through which members can buy, every quarter, the best fiction and non-fiction from a wide range of British publishing houses, mostly in paperback, always at discount.

To receive our latest catalogue, or for information on The Women's Press Book Club, send a large SAE to:

The Sales Department
The Women's Press Ltd
34 Great Sutton Street London EC1V 0LQ
Tel: 020 7251 3007 Fax: 020 7608 1938
www.the-womens-press.com

Alma Fritchley
Chicken Feed
The second Letty Campbell mystery

When Letty's lover Anne sets off for a US-wide lecture tour,
Letty prepares for a mournful few weeks alone on the farm
with only her chickens for company. But her peace is
shattered by the arrival of a strange woman in her kitchen with
a wild and appealing five-year-old child. Before she knows it,
their troubles are hers and Letty is caught up in a sequence of
rapid, outrageous and dangerous events. Why has charismatic
lesbian politician Sita Joshi suddenly disappeared? How come
Letty's gorgeous ex-lover Julia has wound up in jail? What has
it got to do with the top lesbian singer recently in town? And
what is on the video tape that turns up in the village and
almost costs Letty her life . . . ?

'A terrific yarn . . . mightily recommended' *Diva*

'This book had me laughing out loud' *Crime Time*

Crime Fiction £5.99
ISBN 0 7043 4692 3

Alma Fritchley
Chicken Out
The third Letty Campbell mystery

When Letty's ancient neighbour, George, dies in suspicious
circumstances, village tongues start to wag. Can it really be
coincidence that George's glamorous niece, Stephanie,
suddenly appeared just hours before George met his death?
And who is the elderly Cousin Flo, who has also turned up out
of the blue?
Trapped into arranging an unusual funeral and struggling
against Stephanie's considerable charms, Letty wishes that
she was not involved. But as a series of dramatic revelations
unfold, she becomes embroiled in a dangerous case
involving mysterious letters, hidden treasures – and a
secret lesbian love affair . . .

'A terrific yarn . . . mightily recommended' *Diva*

Crime Fiction £6.99
ISBN 0 7043 4619 2

Alma Fritchley
Chicken Shack
The long-awaited fourth Letty Campbell mystery

Mourning the end of a relationship, Letty Campbell, chicken
farmer par excellence, turns her hand to a spot of property
dealing. Aided and abetted by her glamorous sidekick Julia,
Letty sells the land she inherited to a Texan outfit who plan to
set up a health farm.
Letty's mother has been busy too, announcing her engagement
to the fabulously wealthy Colonel Thompson. But when her
mother starts receiving mysterious phone calls, Letty wonders
what skeletons are rattling in the Thompson family closet.
Meanwhile, back at the health farm, Letty finds plenty to
distract her. But is the sleepy Yorkshire village of Calderton
ready for colonic irrigation and 'stunt' aerobics? And what is
the connection between a freak accident, an escaped prisoner,
and a load of filthy lucre . . .

'Alma Fritchley gets better and better' *Eve's Back*

'A talent to watch' *Crime Time*

Crime Fiction £6.99
ISBN 0 7043 4686 9

Manda Scott
Hen's Teeth
A Kellen Stewart crime thriller

Shortlisted for the Orange Prize for Fiction
and the First Blood Award

Midnight in Glasgow. A bad time to be faced with a dead body.
Especially if the body in question is your ex-lover and the
woman grieving at her bedside used to be your friend. Add a
corpse packed with Temazepam, a genetic engineer with a
strange interest in chickens and a killer on the loose with a
knife, and you have all the reasons you need to walk away and
never come back.
Except that it's Bridget who's dead and she has always
deserved better than that. For Dr Kellen Stewart, ex-medic,
ex-lover and ex-friend, a simple call for help rapidly twists
into a tangled web of death and deceit . . .
Hen's Teeth is an extraordinary, powerful, tough crime
thriller that marks the arrival of a superb new writer.

'Eloquent, excellent . . . A new voice for a new
world and it's thrilling' **Fay Weldon**

Crime Fiction £5.99
ISBN 0 7043 4685 0